IT'S ONLY A GAME

It's only a Game

Kids' Football:
25 Years on a Touchline

ANDREW CHRISTOPHERS

T

Troubador Publishing Ltd
Unit E2 Airfield Business Park
Harrison Road, Market Harborough
Leicestershire LE16 7UL
Tel: 0116 279 2299
Email: books@troubador.co.uk
Web: www.troubador.co.uk

ISBN 9781836282068

British Library Cataloguing in Publication Data.
A catalogue record for this book is available from the British Library.

Printed and bound by CPI Group (UK) Ltd, Croydon, CR0 4YY
Typeset in 10pt Avenir Next by Troubador Publishing Ltd, Leicester, UK

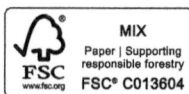

*To all those who have shared my touchline journey –
from Hampton Rangers, NPL Youth and beyond – and
all those who work in grassroots football, giving up
their time and investing their emotions in service of
the beautiful game.*

Contents

"What happens on the football field matters, not in the way that food matters, but as poetry does to some people and alcohol does to others: it engages the personality. It has conflict and beauty, and when those two qualities are present together in something offered for public appraisal, they represent much of what I take to be art. The people own this art in the way they can never own any form of music, theatre, literature or religion."

– *The Football Man* by Arthur Hopcroft

INTRODUCTION

"I can't believe it; I can't believe it. Football, bloody hell!"

So said Sir Alex Ferguson after Manchester United's dramatic Champions League victory over Bayern Munich in stoppage time in 1999. But that emotional roller coaster of football does not just exist at the pinnacle of the beautiful game.

In fact, kids' football has a wonderfully compelling sub-culture all of its own. The grassroots of the game is where the hard yards are put in – and where the camaraderie and comic can become interchangeable. I'm grateful for Jim White's fabulous book *You'll Win Nothing With Kids*, which helped inspire me to write this one.

I found myself on the touchline of kids' football for 25 years. And I wrote a match report for many of those years. So, once I hung up my journalistic boots, I found I had a rich treasure trove of memories to reactivate.

What a journey those 25 years turned out to be. Thrilling, devastating, rewarding, demanding, and above all, just utterly compelling. The players, the personalities, the friendships, the fallings out – what a series of stories there are to tell! The shared endeavour was the catalyst or super glue that held us all together, and the shared experiences were electric. Funny at times, tragic at others, but never dull or boring.

Kids' football, bloody hell!

One important rider, before I launch into telling these stories. I have attributed real names to everyone in this book. Football and football clubs are all about people and personalities. So it seemed rude not to do so. But this is my story and recollections, so it is, of course, told from my perspective. And as the late Queen once skillfully observed, "Recollections may differ". I therefore apologise in advance for any offence caused or factual inaccuracies, of which there will no doubt be many. After all, who wants the truth to get in the way of telling a good story?!

CHAPTER 1

SETTING THE SCENE

"Football fans aren't here to solve the world, we're here to get away from the world." – Pod on The Tyne.

I was at St James's Park on the last day of the 2022-23 season, in the Gallowgate End, where I have a season ticket these days with my older son, Jack. Eddie Howe had worked miracles, and, having saved us from relegation the season before, had now guided us to a fourth-place finish, and Champions League qualification.

All the players, staff and their families came onto the pitch at the end, to celebrate with the fans. And there was Miguel Almirón's tiny little son, 'Mini Miggy', who must only have been four years old, kicking a ball down the pitch, and into the net in front of us, cheered on by 50,000 Geordies. Lads and dads and football. It all came flooding back to me. I had so many memories. And most of them were good ones, too. I had to capture those experiences, and write them down.

⚽

I guess I've always had a bit of an obsession with football. It started when I was 7 or 8, and wanted to become a goalkeeper. So I followed Gordon Banks, England's then No 1, and became a Stoke City fan. Many years later, I met and then married

Helen, a true-born Geordie. So the lure of Newcastle United came knocking. Quite loudly, in fact. Football is a religion in the North-East. I soon switched my allegiances, and became one of that forever-condemned group of football fans, who can never be seen as 'true' or 'proper'. But at least I'm not a glory hunter. The Toon's last major trophy remains the Fairs Cup in 1969, when I was still a Stoke supporter.

I never indoctrinated my own children, or at least I hope I didn't. Jack started kicking a football (and wearing Newcastle and England shirts) soon after he could walk. Mia arrived next, and, poor soul, she got all the hand-me-down strips. I think she quite liked the shirts, although she had no interest in actually kicking a football. Indeed, she was always placed in goal (wearing ludicrously large goalie gloves) whenever Jack's friends came round to play. Then, several years later, Will was born. At first he wasn't really taken by the round ball. But once he drew Wayne Rooney in our family sweepstake for the Euro Finals in 2004, he suddenly saw the light. And the rest is history.

So with first Jack and then Will, I embarked on an odyssey into kids' football, from Under 6 or 7 level right up to Under 17's or 18's – and not just once, but two times over. For 25 years, kids' football became the pulsebeat of my weekends, and my weeks too. It was my release from work, and it punctuated both my working and my family life. There's a great line in T. S. Eliot's poem, *The Love Song of J. Alfred Prufrock*, that reads, *"I have measured out my life in coffee spoons."* It's a reflection about growing old, and realising you have spent the majority of your life performing mundane tasks. Kids' football is how I measured out those 25 years – although it was anything but mundane.

I had two long spells with the clubs that my boys played for. Jack was with Hampton Rangers for 12 years, and then Will was with NPL Youth for 13 years. More about both clubs will follow shortly. But Hampton Rangers played in what was then the West Surrey Youth League, while our NPL Youth team competed in the Epsom & Ewell League, and latterly the Surrey Youth League. Both teams played at decent levels – Premier or Premier Elite level – and both provided plenty of ups, downs and all-round entertainment, both on and off the pitch.

Hampton Rangers was, in many ways, a rehearsal for me for the NPL years that were to follow. Rangers was then a much smaller and less established club. Fund raising was essential, and the club's very existence was threatened at times. But we still managed to reach Cup Finals, go on tours to Spain, and attract a manager who has gone on to coach at Premier League level. NPL is part of a much bigger sports club, based in Teddington, so the scale and organisation were on a completely different level.

⚽

My role with both teams was the same. Nothing as grand as Chairman or Sporting Director, and nothing as important as Manager or Coach. I was just the chief cheerleader, in charge of team and touchline 'glue', and also off-field organisation: communication, fixtures, training arrangements and end-of-season tours. I never wanted to cross the white line, or have responsibility for what happened on the pitch, because that was specialist territory and where the serious stuff happened. But I was more than happy to do everything up to that point.

And, although I have pursued a career in marketing, I guess I am also a frustrated sports journalist at heart. So, at least by the NPL years, by which stage we had internet and email, I became the self-appointed match reporter too. It was fun to write a brief piece once a week, to capture that week's match, and the resultant emotions. And I've ended up with over 250 match reports, spanning those 13 years. (For this reason, my NPL memories and stories are more top-of-mind and prevalent than my Hampton Rangers ones).

And then, suddenly, one day the roller coaster stopped. The boys had grown up, and left home – transferring their footballing allegiances to university sides instead; how could they?! There was no real need or opportunity for my touchline presence anymore. But how could I replace it? What about those withdrawal symptoms on Sunday mornings? What on earth would I do? Those unpalatable words "the Sainsbury's shop" began echoing in my ears...

As I look back now over those reports, which chronicle so much hope, excitement and emotion, I can laugh at some, shudder at others, and overall re-enjoy the ride. But I can also re-live those 25 years on a touchline with a tad more perspective – which was in short supply when everything was 'live'. And there are one or two nuggets which warrant reproducing. Like these closing thoughts after our last ever game:

"With the mums singing One Direction on the touchline, I'm left thinking that *Whole Lot of History* could be the soundtrack of the last 13 years with this NPL team. Our manager, Steven Bates, then suggests we could publish his NPL footballing diaries under the title *War & Peace*... It's what Sunday morning football is all about!"

CONTEXT & PROTAGONISTS

FOUNDED 1969

Hampton Rangers Junior Football Club, located in the heart of Hampton in Middlesex, was formed in 1969 by Denis Chaplin and local policeman PC Peter Rice, to help get children off the street. The initial ethos, still true today, was "football for all, regardless of ability." The club's most famous ex-player is Peter Rhoades-Brown, who went on to play for Chelsea, making 96 appearances as a left winger between 1979 and 1984, and then Oxford United. The club is thriving today under the leadership of Billy Martin, with success being measured in terms of participation, not just results. The vision is to make football fun, whether formally or casually, for male and female players alike, ranging from 2- to 90-year-olds.

Denis Chaplin - co-founder and Honorary Life President of Hampton Rangers JFC. Denis, by then in his 60's, started up our team when the boys were aged 6 or 7 - and (with a little help) took them right through to age 17 or 18. A local kids' football legend, aka Mr Hampton Rangers.

Eduardo Rubio - arrived from Spain and Valencia to start his coaching career with Hampton Rangers, while completing a Masters in Sports Psychology at Roehampton University. Once he mastered the English tongue, Edu brought unmatched enthusiasm, commitment and enjoyment to the role. He now plies his trade in the Premier League!

NPL Youth Football Club is based in Teddington, Middlesex, with NPL standing for the National Physical Laboratory. The sports club was founded in 1905, and the first football at NPL was played in 1912. NPL is an FA Charter Standard 2-Star accredited football club, affiliated with Middlesex FA, and with direct links into NPL senior teams and adult football. There are 26 teams for boys and girls aged from 7 through to 18 years of age. Current £25m Brighton and Denmark midfielder Matt O'Riley started his career with NPL U8's, before joining Fulham's Academy and then playing for Celtic. NPL aims to give youth members the opportunity to play competitive football in a safe, controlled and friendly environment, under the supervision of FA Qualified Coaches. It aims to help young players find challenges, enjoyment and fun, and learn about teamwork, as they practice and play football.

Steven Bates – played football to a semi-professional level in his youth, but was always destined to excel as a coach. Charismatic and colourful, 'Batesie' has always been a heart and soul coach, fully committed both technically and emotionally as well. Never dull, never boring, and capable of rousing team talks to inspire his players, making you laugh – or cry.

CHAPTER 2

WHERE IT ALL BEGAN

"The journey of a thousand miles begins with one step."
– Lao Tzu.

Jack must have been five years old. He wasn't well, but his friends had told him about a new junior football team that was forming, and interested players and parents were invited down to Oldfield Road in Hampton. Never mind the illness, the lure of the beautiful game was too strong.

But it was an inauspicious start. We all had to scramble under a fence and through a hedge to find the training pitch. Little did I know what we had just started, and what was going to unfold over the next 25 years. On the other side of the hedge, there was Denis to greet us. An avuncular man in his sixties, smartly dressed in a Hampton Rangers training top, and brimming with a mixture of contained excitement alongside seen-it-all-before cynicism. But more of Denis later.

It was similar with Will: back from school with a note, amidst great excitement from him and his friends. A new team forming, new players wanted. But he already had a bit of an advantage. There had been some early small-sided 'training' sessions on Saturday mornings, run by parent volunteers. They had a massive 'man of the match' award, like a golden boot, which went to the most inspired performer each week.

A non-footballing boy won it for "running into space" – a great euphemism for not wanting to touch the ball. How to turn a negative into a positive. A vital early lesson in understanding kids' football.

⚽

The early days with Rangers were not exactly heady. There was a Portakabin for a clubhouse, but I think a shipping container might be a more accurate description: there were certainly no windows. That's where Denis used to gather his young charges for one of his famed motivational team talks – where the lack of air and prevalence of smelly socks, sweat and football boots was not exactly built for motivation. I had to take Mia along with me, when I was looking after both of our young children, and unfortunately Denis's 'shed' put her off the beautiful game for more than 20 years. It wasn't until she met her football-teaching partner in later years that she deigned to visit a clubhouse again – and I can hardly blame her.

The training pitch wasn't much better, either. Filled with giant fox and rabbit holes, it was just asking for twisted if not broken ankles. Then one night at 'training', a herd of wild horses suddenly appeared out of nowhere, and came galloping across the pitch. Where on earth did they come from, and what would the FA's health and safety committees have to say about it? I just recall 16 or so rather shell-shocked seven-year-olds diving for cover into Denis's shed.

⚽

When you start volunteering in kids' football, one of the great fears you have is whether your own kids are going to be good enough. Both my boys were very similar footballers in many ways. Both developed into ball-playing centre backs, both very two-footed, but neither really relishing the crunching Norman Hunter-like tackle, and neither blessed with great pace either. But their reading of the game (having watched as well as played so much football) often more than made up for that.

Jack was always confident off the pitch, and that extended to his on-field presence too. But he could also be head-strong. When he was only 7 or 8, he had a bit of a strop with Denis, the then-manager, and handed him back his selection letter. He was promptly (and rightly) stripped of the captaincy, and Alex, a rather more level-headed individual, took over the armband.

When Eduardo later coached the team, I remember one half-time team talk almost exclusively directed one-on-one to Jack. Edu told me he realised that if he could get Jack's head right and have him playing for the team, then the rest would follow suit.

Jack has continued to love the game, both playing and watching. He plays football in the way he embraces life: full-on, vocal and with an infectious enthusiasm. He ended up playing 12 full years for Hampton Rangers, through many bad times, and with the occasional highlight too.

Will was much less confident initially, and I worried about his robustness and physical resilience. He started as a striker, and had a knack of finishing well – but he could also drift out of games, and get muscled off the ball. When he was substituted, for the third time in one particular game (admittedly only aged 8 or so), he promptly burst into tears, and I wondered whether he'd last as a footballer.

But he grew into a highly accomplished and confident 6-feet-5-inch centre back, a commanding presence in the team, and with the calmness to captain it too (unlike his big brother!) Will played 13 full years for NPL Youth, evolving and developing as a player as the team improved and progressed. That willowy one-touch striker blossomed into an assured and ball-playing centre back – who was also always likely to score a few goals as well.

CHAPTER 3

SENSE OF BELONGING

"What is a club in any case? Not the buildings or the directors or the people who are paid to represent it. It's not the television contracts, get-out clauses, marketing departments or executive boxes. It's the noise, the passion, the feeling of belonging, the pride in your city. It's a small boy clambering up stadium steps for the very first time, gripping his father's hand, gawping at that hallowed stretch of turf beneath him and, without being able to do a thing about it, falling in love."

This iconic quote is, perhaps unsurprisingly, from Sir Bobby Robson. Bobby knew a thing or two about club football, having managed at Ipswich Town, PSV, Sporting Lisbon, Porto, Barcelona and Newcastle United, as well of course as being England's national team manager.

Bobby also knew how to talk, and how to talk at length. I remember being in a bar in Newcastle after we had beaten Manchester United 4-3 back in 2001. Bobby came onto Sky Sports TV and was asked about the game. The whole bar fell silent, you could hear a pin drop. "Well," he began, "it was a right Bobby Dazzler of a game, wasn't it?" He proceeded to talk through all of the 7 goals in infinite detail, with everyone in the bar listening attentively, hanging on his every syllable. The Sky Sports reporter finally got to speak again. "We would have asked Bobby a second question, but we're only on air until 7:30 tonight!"

⚽

But Bobby perfectly encapsulates the emotion, the pride and the belonging of club football in his wonderful quote, above. Having spent a career in marketing, I have had ample opportunity to try to understand human behaviour and motivation. Having a sense of belonging is one of the greatest drivers of human happiness, and over the years this has been played out in many adverts, none more so than in the beer market. Years ago, John Smith's used a memorable ditty, of three men heading off to the pub: "Got a mate called Brown and a mate called Jones, and we're off to meet a mate called Smith." And more recently, Budweiser revamped their iconic "Wassup" campaign; a celebration of the sense of human belonging. So united is this particular tribe, they even communicate with their own non-verbal language.

And football is no different. A shared passion, belief and identity, with teams and supporters united with shared team colours, shirts, scarfs and logos. I used to marvel when younger brothers turned up in replica NPL kits on the touchline!

A club is defined as being a collection of people, brought together for a common cause. That's what I loved about those Sunday mornings: the democracy of the touchline. It doesn't matter whether you're a judge, a plumber, an accountant or a bus driver during the week. On Sunday mornings, the cross-section of society is all united together, believing in a common cause. Shared experiences, shared emotions and a shared sense of belonging. Us against them, our tribe against their tribe.

Maybe the great football managers really understand the power of unity. The late and legendary Liverpool manager Bill

Shankly said, "A football club is a holy trinity – the players, the manager and the supporters." And Liverpool's own anthem, *"You'll Never Walk Alone"*, certainly captures the very essence of belonging. More recently, while guiding Leicester City to a highly unlikely Premier League title, Claudio Ranieri said, "This is a club that is showing the world what can be achieved through spirit and determination. Twenty-six players. Twenty-six different brains. But one heart."

In my experience, team sports are all about collaboration. It's why, during my working life when I was hiring, I always looked for team sports involvement across people's CV's. Ironic, really, because although I played school 1st XI football as a rather average right back, I was always more accomplished as a middle to long-distance runner. If I wasn't listening in class, my German teacher would always call me to attention, "Dreaming again, are we Christophers? The loneliness of the long-distance runner?!"

But I love the team dynamic of a football club – almost as much as I love a Bobby Robson quote. "Sign good people, not just good players," the great man said – and he was right. Denis always said he had been lucky with his parents and players over the years, and maybe he had. But I think you also make your own luck, by who you recruit into a club, and by how you treat people as well. Denis reaped what he had sown.

Steven, our NPL manager, also brought in some great people over the years (both players and parents), and it was rewarding to see how well the team dynamic could grow and develop. One match report notes the new players and parents commenting on how easily they fitted in and felt welcomed; how much they enjoyed being part of the team; how few egos there were, with no 'star player' syndrome; and how funny the goalkeeper was... (more of him and his father later!) The All Blacks New Zealand rugby team value their team ethic above everything else, stating in the book, *Legacy*, "A player who makes the team great is better than a great player."

I think this is why we kept our teams together for so long. A Cup Final programme from 2016 notes that, having come together at U7 level, our NPL team was then in its 12th season – and we still had 5 graduates from the Class of 2004; boys who started with the club aged 5, and were still playing together at 18 years old. Manchester United Class of '92, eat your heart out! Who was it that said, if you want loyalty in football, then just buy a dog?!

I guess the sense of belonging culminated in our last ever game. We won a League and Cup double for the second year running – dubbed The Double Double – and I counted 44 people in that final celebratory touchline picture: players, parents, grandparents, coaches, uncles, aunts, brothers and sisters. A celebration of the unity, democracy and shared passion of kids' football. And the reason why, now 10 years or more on, those bonds still exist. Those shared experiences run deep.

CHAPTER 4

OVER-INVESTED & OVER-EMOTIONAL

"Some people think football is a matter of life and death. I can assure you, it's much more serious than that." - Bill Shankly.

It's sometimes difficult to fathom, in the professional game, how 11 strangers kicking a ball around can have such a ludicrously significant impact on our mood and emotions. People we don't know and who wouldn't know us can somehow influence and effect our whole lives. But throw in the personal connection that's inherent in kids' football, and the emotions can become even stronger. If your professional team is doing badly, you can always try to step back from the pain a little, and immerse yourself in other things. But not when your own flesh and blood are involved: then there's no escaping.

My weekends were always gauged by three key football results: Jack's team, Will's team and Newcastle United. These games took on a ridiculous importance and significance. Three defeats, and I'd be moping about and miserable the following week. A mixture of wins and defeats, or a draw or two, I could just about live with. But occasionally, just very occasionally, we would register three straight wins out of three. It didn't happen very often. And even less so, if it was an away 'treble' of wins. But sometimes it did. And what a feeling that was. The madness, the gladness – and the celebratory beers!

Looking back, I don't know whether it was mild obsession or full-on addiction. But the mental space that kids' football commanded in my life was bordering on the insane. I would check the league table several times a day, and all through the week; (as if it was going to change, from one match to the next?) I would be ringing round everyone after Sunday morning pitch inspections (this was the days before WhatsApp or group text messaging), confirming that the match was still on.

I would lie awake at night, worrying about player injuries. I wasn't counting sheep, but rather calf, quad, groin and concussion conditions. I was agitating about conflicting priorities. We began to have players getting county trials and call-ups, so we would miss them for vital fixtures. Could we get the league to re-arrange our games? People were away, for half-term, skiing or holidays – perhaps not unreasonably.

Some boys had other sporting commitments (how dare they?) such as hockey, cricket or athletics, plus (in one case) an international call-up for the England Korfball team. I had to look it up: it's a Dutch sport that's a cross between netball and basketball, played with teams of eight players, four male and four female. It was first played in 1902, and an Olympic demonstration sport in 1920 and 1928. But it was going to cost us our centre forward, and that was all that mattered.

Our NPL goalkeeper, Max, had tickets to a Stormzy concert, so told the manager he couldn't play in a key title-deciding game. I was distraught – and at the time, I didn't even know who Stormzy was. The manager lectured him about his priorities – but I think he probably got them right, and went to the concert.

Then, in the later years, there was a devastating phone call from Will's school, where the football coach wanted him to stop playing Sunday league football, and to prioritise school football instead, training and Saturday 1ˢᵗ XI matches. I was a broken man. 25 years on a touchline, and my whole little world was beginning to crumble and collapse around me.

At least I managed to deflect some of the pain with the match report, on that particular occasion. "It's been quite a week on Planet Football. First Big Sam [Allardyce] gets the boot. 'Entrapment' wins. Luckily Batesie was only offered a Big Mac bung and not the £400k! Then Newcastle snatch a very late victory out of the jaws of defeat against Norwich. With goals in the 95ᵗʰ & 96ᵗʰ minutes. And Rafa gets a big bear-hug from our centre forward [Aleksandar Mitrović]. Leaving me wondering who's going to pick up Batesie if we win The Treble. Especially given the Big Mac. And then Will gets his collar felt by his school coach about the amount of football he's playing. Which leaves me feeling like Big Sam and wondering what to do with my life."

⚽

I guess I just cared too much – often more than the boys who were playing – and attached a disproportionate importance to it all. But I wasn't the only one.

Big Adam was the father to NPL's goalkeeper, Max. A larger-than-life character on the touchline (and off it too) and a constant supporter, whatever the weather, Adam was the master of touchline banter and the one-liner.

But I remember standing in the carpark with Steven and Big Adam at the end of one of the summer tournaments, and all three of us talking for ages. We couldn't end the conversation, because we couldn't face the fact that the season had finished.

We weren't ready and we didn't want the pain of the close season, and the prospect of a whole summer with no kids' football.

It all reminds me of the Woody Allen quote at the beginning of the film *Annie Hall*. *"Remember that old joke - you know, a guy walks into a psychiatrist's office and says, hey doc, my brother's crazy! He thinks he's a chicken. Then the doc says, why don't you turn him in? Then the guy says, I would - but I need the eggs. I guess that's how I feel about relationships. They're totally crazy, irrational, and absurd, but we keep going through it - because we need the eggs."*

Kids' football is addictive, like a drug. It's superb, frustrating, crazy, irrational and absurd. But I guess we all keep going through it, because we too need the eggs!

⚽

Gary Neville knows a thing or two about footballing wisdom and philosophy. He summarises the appeal of the game as follows: *"Football is about emotions. Humour, disappointment, anxiety, sheer joy, sheer sadness. It's all of the emotions you experience at different points throughout the week, but it's jammed into 90 minutes. To me, the beauty of football is that roller coaster. Very few things in life will make you feel like that."*

I'm sure many of us can empathise with these feelings. Unbridled joy, alongside heartache and pain. And it's those highs and lows of the football roller coaster that fuel the addiction. After every low, you're just desperate to get back on the horse again, and experience some joy. And after every high, you just love the feeling, and want to replicate it again, the following week.

Liam was a tenacious right back, who made up in determination what he lacked in speed and skill. He'd played for nearly 10 long seasons, doggedly and at times brilliantly, but never earning the plaudits of some of his more famed and feted team mates. Then, one Sunday morning, he goes up for a corner, rising majestically (like a flying kipper). And somehow, with a ricochet or a shoulder involved, he manages to 'head' the ball into the net – and score his first ever goal. Cue scenes of pandemonium and wild celebrations. We were still calming down his father, Graham, six weeks later.

When we reached our first ever Cup Final, it felt a bit like Newcastle recently reaching the Carabao Cup Final, their first for over 20 years. The match report captures some of those feelings. "It was exhilarating today, and it was emotional too. It was emotional before the match: Big Adam's motivational text to Max read: 'Do it for you, do it for your team mates, and most importantly, do it because you can!' It was emotional during the match, which hung on a knife edge for most of the 120 pulsating minutes. And it was emotional afterwards, with Steven saying he's never been more proud of his team, before shaking the hands of all 16 players individually. This team has waited 11 long years to reach a Cup final, and we've now finally done it. And we did it through courage, hunger, self-belief, commitment and some outstanding footballing ability as well. Take a bow, NPL Youth." I can't now remember whether it was a game we even won or lost!

⚽

And then there were the lows: not just the results, but the other incidents as well. When the kids were very young, emotions and expectations could of course run high. We were being managed at the time by an amiable taxi driver called John (when Steven was unable to be in the dugout) and he was doing his best to keep the 8-year-old boys motivated. He also had to rotate his players, to ensure everyone had a fair amount of time on the pitch, not on the bench. And it was a delicate balancing act: kids' football managers need a degree in diplomacy, alongside their coaching badges.

But when John substituted his own son just once too often, Kieran just lost it. Normally a quiet and law-abiding kid, he had finally had enough. Angrily, he burst into tears, and tore off his shirt, hurling it to the ground. And then he was off. There must have been 6 other football pitches at the God-forsaken Nescot Sports Ground we were playing at, plus a few hedges to get through as well. But he just kept going – Forrest Gump-like. And John went after him, his voice getting higher and higher as he screamed, "Kieran! Kieran! Come back! Come back NOW!" It was the last we ever saw of them both.

The boys were slightly older, and Steven was back in the dugout, when we were playing away at Alexandra Park in Epsom. Again, pitch-time was the issue. We had a tricky and skilful little player called Luca, and his motor-mouth was more than a match for his dancing feet. Chirpy when he was up, but as we came to find out, less so when he was down. He took exception to being subbed off, and famously called his manager a "knobhead" – a somewhat controversial observation, but one which his mother fully endorsed. So unfortunately, that was the end of those dancing feet – although the infamous "Luca-gate" story lived on for many seasons to come.

And of course, the highs and the lows sometimes became interchangeable. There were moments when you were standing in the rain, after witnessing five straight defeats, wondering why you do it all. And then you get a completely unexpected and scintillating 5-0 away win – and life is just wonderful again. Keep taking the tablets!

Maybe motivational quotes are an over-investment in kids' football, but I had to try some out. How could we get into the boys' heads, and find some psychological advantage? After a disappointingly half-hearted display, when we needed to show more desire, I turned to Ian Thorpe, the Australian swimmer, aka The Thorpedo. "Losing is not coming second. Losing is getting out of the water knowing you could have done better."

When we needed more effort, I found inspiration from the former Brazilian footballer Kaká: "I can have the skill, the ambition, the talent, the technique and the desire. But without sweat I have nothing." This was actually a line from a Gatorade ad at the time, which went on to declare, "When you give everything, Gatorade gives it back." If only our boys could be a little more Gatorade.

And as a one-time semi-professional footballer, whose playing days were taken away from him far too early due to injury, Steven also weighed in with his own form of motivation for his team. He found this from NFL player Robert Mathis, who was suspended from playing for violating a performance-enhancing drugs policy. So he left this message in his locker for his team mates:

"Athletes: Don't take the sport you play for granted. Every time you play, you better be damn thankful that you get to do something you love. Don't show up to practice complaining about not wanting to be there; you're there hopefully because you love it. Work hard every moment. If you're not working hard, you don't deserve to play. Play every practice or game like it's your last, because it very well could be. When you finally reach the day that you can't play, and you can only watch, then you will know how much you love something that you once took for granted."

⚽

Were we expecting too much of our junior charges? Probably. But we couldn't help ourselves. We had to dream big. With a title run-in beckoning one season, I noted that there was a sign up in the NPL car park that talks about "A glimpse at the history of the National Physical Laboratory." I mused whether we could write a new chapter of that history over the next few months.

I drew parallels with Newcastle United, recalling that horrible sense of *déjà vu* dating back to the 1995-96 season, when we were 12 points clear of Manchester United at Christmas, but still lost the league. I urged Steven not to do a Kevin Keegan, but to "Keep calm and carry on." I also tried to tell myself, it's only kids' football, isn't it? But it's the hope that kills you, right?

I am reminded of that brilliant scene at the end of the film *Parenthood* with Steve Martin. Martin plays Gil Buckman, who is coaching his non-sporting son, Kevin, in their Little League baseball team. After Kevin has dropped several catches, one final one goes up into the air, with the match depending on it. Somehow, miraculously, Kevin falls over and takes the catch. His dad goes mad, whooping and celebrating up and down the touchline, while Kevin is mobbed by his super-happy team mates. And later on, that evening, Gil reflects on the event with his wife, Karen.

Gil: *"I am still high from the Little League game."*
Karen: *"Isn't that demented? That a grown man's happiness depends on whether a nine-year-old catches a pop-up?"*
Gil: *"What if he missed?"*

Karen: "But he didn't."

Gil: "But he could have."

Karen: "But he didn't, Gil. You threw him a million pop-ups in the backyard. You cut the odds considerably."

That's what we all went through and were hoping for every Sunday morning, over those 25 years. The anticipation, the significance, the elation. Many grown men's happiness depended on it. So, and with the glorious benefit of hindsight, maybe we did put a bit too much pressure on our nine-year-olds!

CHAPTER 5

THE GAFFERS

"He made the people happy."

These five simple words are inscribed beneath an iconic statue in Liverpool of Bill Shankly, the legendary football manager. They summarise what it means to be a football manager, at whatever level. The responsibility, but the opportunity too. You are conductor of the orchestra, the beating heart of a team or club. And you can have a disproportionate influence over many people's moods and feelings.

But if the manager's job isn't easy in Premier League football, then it's certainly not easy in kids' football either. Sure, there may not be the media scrutiny or financial implications. But there is plenty of other scrutiny, and opinions galore, from which the manager is rarely shielded.

I once (and only once) took on the manager's role myself, when all the much better qualified candidates were away. We were playing away in East Sheen, against a much better team. I started our big centre forward (Big Ben) at centre back, hoping we could keep the score to 0-0 at half-time. The plan failed spectacularly, as we came in 4-0 down. I tried to motivate the boys, saying that with Big Ben back up front for the second half, the opposition would be terrified. We lost 8-0 and I sacked myself in the car park straight afterwards. Never again!

There is also the perennial debate about whether youth football should be about winning or about participating. Do you 'move on' your weaker players, however loyal and committed they may be, and bring in stronger players? And what about the ongoing dilemma of 'minutes on the pitch'? Do you rotate all boys to give them an equal chance and equal 'pitch-time', or do you favour the better players, and try to win the match? Decisions, decisions – and usually with big consequences as well.

Boys inevitably recognise who the better players are, even from a very young age. And the true team players would probably rather be part of a winning team, even if it means playing less time themselves, than feel they had let the side down, because the manager has felt obliged to play them.

But equally, nobody should come out to play, and never get onto the pitch. The curse of the unused substitute. OK, maybe in Premier League football – but not at grassroots level. In an Under 9 game, Steven once left one poor child on the touchline for the whole game. He kept waiting to bring him on, getting him warmed up and ready. But the game was just too tight, and Steven didn't want to risk losing it. "5 minutes." But 5 minutes came and went. The boy was stripped and ready for action, but the match hung on a knife-edge. Every time the ball went out of play, the boy moved forward. But Steven held him back again. And time finally ran out.

The player and his parents were understandably not happy. So he was made captain next week. Steven even gave him the Manager's Player of the Year award at the end of the season, to acknowledge his mistake. But into the next season, when the same boy decided he was quitting the club, I've never seen Steven accept a resignation so rapidly: quick, he said, before he changes his mind.

My first experience of a kids' football manager was the wonderfully genial and ageing Denis Chaplin at Hampton Rangers. Denis had been an accountant by trade, and had co-founded Hampton Rangers as a junior football club 30 years previously, back in 1969. He worked alongside a policeman, PC Rice (or Copper Rice, as Denis always called him), leading a local initiative to try to get kids off the streets, and do something more worthwhile. And their legacy has lived on to this day, with free Saturday morning sessions for ages 2-3, and the ongoing ethos of "Football for all, regardless of ability."

Denis was well into his sixties when our team was formed, and he had come back to take one final team through the age groups. He had coached two boys from the Veasey family, and was very good friends with all the family. So when their third and final son, Simon, was at a football-playing age, Denis vowed to do it all again: one last hurrah!

Denis's enthusiasm never wavered, though his patience was no longer what it had once been. His team talks became legendary, ironically named as "motivational"; Denis could always turn a positive into a negative – though we loved him for it. "Stop bunching," he would scream at the boys, as they all followed the ball – a phrase my own son Jack found himself shouting at kids when he became a teacher, many years later. And Denis had been around too long to take any shit from mouthy young boys too: "Stop piss-arsing about", he was fond of saying. If he had an opinion to offer, Denis didn't stand on ceremony or political correctness. When Jack brought two of his school friends down for a trial, Denis liked one of them, but said of the other, "Don't bother bringing the fat lad back again!"

As Denis's years advanced, we realised we needed to bring in a younger person with more energy to manage the ongoing coaching. One of the mums worked at Roehampton University, and she advertised for Sports Science students. We found a coach, Craig, who came and joined us for one season. But we then struck gold, finding a young Spanish coach, whose English was still developing, called Eduardo Rubio. Edu had nearly made it as a professional at Valencia, as a ball-playing centre back – and now, aged 20 or so, he was looking to develop his coaching career in the UK. The Spanish Revolution was about to begin.

⚽

What an addition Edu proved to be. Humble, respectful and hard-working from the start, he forged a great working relationship with Denis – father-son, or maybe even grandfather-grandson at times. And he was a massive hit with the boys as well, gaining their trust and respect instantly, while also building a strong rapport, being only 5 or 6 years older than them.

As Edu's English developed, his coaching skills really came to the fore. He had a maturity and drive well beyond his years, and was just brilliant with teenagers and adults alike, including one particularly high-profile parent: Brian Barwick, who was Chief Executive of the Football Association at the time. Edu was our team coach from 2004 to 2008, taking us to two Cup Finals, and his training, coaching, motivating and organising were executed with real energy, passion and enthusiasm. He gave the boys great self-belief, ensuring they got real enjoyment from their football.

Edu always said, even in those early days, that one day he wanted to manage in the Premier League. While I admired his ambition, I wasn't sure it could ever become a reality. But he was as good as his word. After spells at The Football Association and Nike Academy, Edu went on to hold coaching roles at Chelsea Academy, MK Dons, Crystal Palace and West Ham women, and was Assistant Head Coach at Crawley Town. Then, in 2022, he joined Julen Lopetegui as First Team Coach at Wolverhampton Wanderers, frequently appearing live on TV in the dugout and on the touchline, as well as at Wolves' press conferences. And he has now moved, with Lopetegui, to become First Team Coach at West Ham United. From Hampton Rangers to the Premier League, in just 15 years. Big kudos, amigo!

⚽

Denis was delighted to have the support of some youthful energy: he and Edu had real mutual respect, and their relationship stretched way beyond football and Hampton Rangers. Another of the dads, Steven Higgins, also put himself forward to help with the coaching. Steven was schooled as a centre back in the best traditions of Doncaster Rovers, with a penchant for Yorkshire pies, and a belief in a coaching clipboard. In those early days, Steven once asked Eduardo if he was sure he was really capable of doing the job!

Steven's son, Ed, was a prolific centre forward and goal scorer. It's difficult to conceal your pride as a parent, but after one game, Steven gathered the boys together for a post-match debrief. It was a commanding 5-0 win, and he went through all the positives, focusing on the defence, the midfield and the attack. Knowing full-well the answer, he then finished with the throw-away rhetorical question, "And… hat-trick, was it, Eddie?"

Andy McLaren, another dad, became the self-appointed goalkeeping coach. We now had a full complement of a coaching team, and the club could progress accordingly.

In later years, we went on two fabulous tours to Spain, organised by Eduardo. Denis delighted in his role as our senior dignitary, and we all dubbed him 'El Presidente'. There is some wonderful video footage of him coming back on the plane from Spain, drinking from the Cup the boys had won, and then being interviewed for his views on the tour. "The boys weren't as bad as I thought they were going to be," was his concluding assessment, in true dead-beat Denis style!

⚽

Denis was one of those supreme givers in life. He had no ego, nor desire for the limelight. He did so much for youth football, founding a club and then coaching hundreds of boys for nearly 40 years. I once tried to enter him for the BBC's Sports Personality of the Year's Unsung Hero award. But, typically of Denis, he refused to sign the entry form, as he didn't want any fuss.

Denis died suddenly, aged 75, a couple of years after our team had finished (with boys moving on to universities or adult football). The *Match of the Day* music was played at his funeral, and what a moving sight it was to see 20 of our team, all suited and booted, paying their respects to the father figure of Hampton Rangers. The local press reported his death with the headline "Coach was Unsung Hero", commenting on his life as a community figure, his ability to bring kids and parents together, and how so many of his players referred to him as Uncle Denis.

Eduardo said at the time, "It's a sad day for those who knew him, and for those who believe in true football values, such as respect, friendship and honesty. Denis represented all those, both on and off the pitch. He'll always be our 'Presidente'." And Maurizio, an Italian whose son had joined the club in the latter years, said, "Denis was a very special concentrate of all that is good and inspiring about football, teamwork and the notion of taking good care of one another. He will be fondly remembered, and our boys are, I think, a bit different – and a bit better – because of him."

We collected money, and funded a memorial bench, which sits pitch-side in Hatherop Park – so Denis can continue to watch over his beloved Hampton Rangers (maybe with the odd cryptic or critical comment). Denis certainly made a massive impact – and he made many people happy as well.

⚽

Colourful might be a word that was invented to describe Steven Bates. 'Batesie' became our NPL manager for most of the 13 years through which we took the team. And what a larger-than-life gaffer he was too. In some ways, more Mike Bassett than Mike Bassett, from the satirical film *England Manager*. The programme notes from one of our Cup Final appearances feature a Meet the Manager section saying, "Our team is managed by the colourful and charismatic Steven Bates, who holds UEFA B License and Level 3 FA Youth Award coaching badges, and is known for his rousing team talks and infectious enthusiasm."

At the start, our NPL team was managed by Adrian Sandy – polite, mild-mannered, courteous and respectful. Little did we know how things would change! Adrian stepped aside after that first year, and three dads threw their hats into the ring: Steven, Barry and Stuart. But there was only ever going to be one winner, and Steven soon took charge – as the most vocal, dedicated and driven of individuals.

But it wasn't all plain sailing. Steven was going through a very difficult split from his partner, with a lot of accusations and counter-accusations. This meant there were times when Steven was not allowed to coach the team, or even be on the touchline. But such was his desire, he would come to away games, and watch through a hole in the hedge, passing on instructions; (a bit like the time José Mourinho was serving a touchline ban at Chelsea, so was smuggled into Stamford Bridge hidden in a laundry basket).

Steven's partner ended up taking his two sons out to live in Canada. But even without a son to coach, he was determined to keep managing the team – and thereby stay in touch with kids the same age as his own son; also in the hope that Joe would come back one day, and be able to re-join the team (which he did). But Steven's health suffered, and he had to have heart surgery, and a pace-maker fitted. He told the story of how he was declared clinically dead for 12 minutes, during which time he found himself playing for Tottenham Hotspur in an FA Cup Final at Wembley. He rose, majestically, at the back post (like a leaping salmon, as one does), to head in the winning goal!

⚽

We had to make other arrangements during Steven's enforced absences, but he never let anyone take his hand off the tiller. During one Under 12 County Cup game away at Inter Ditton, Steven was still lying recovering in a hospital bed. He delivered his pre-match team talk from a mobile phone on speaker mode – and had the boys so pumped up and motivated that they played out of their skin.

Such acts generated extreme loyalty from his players and parents alike. One boy, Ellis, a supremely gifted footballer, didn't have a father in his life at the time – so, with Steven's own son away, the two of them struck up a great rapport: a father without a son, and a son without a father. And, when Steven was being forced to step back a bit, I remember one particularly dominant and forceful parent, Tim, showing unqualified belief in him as a coach, telling the NPL Chairman: "I want Steven to coach my son."

Steven always wore his heart on his sleeve, acting with honesty and integrity as he dealt with difficult personal circumstances, winning respect and admiration from players and parents alike, both as a coach but also as a person. He delivered some rousing team talks over the years, which had the parents (as well as the boys) willing to spill blood for the cause.

At one tournament, he gave an impassioned address to a new signing about "what it means to wear the blue and yellow shirt of NPL." When the team were nervous before a big Cup game, and the supporters were wearing down their fingernails, Steven would empathise and diffuse the situation, saying he hadn't had so many butterflies since his first date. When we were out-muscled and physically intimidated, he would honestly assess, "When it comes to push, we got pushed". And he was famed for his footballing wisdom, such as "Goals don't move", when our centre forward missed the target.

I remember a headline in the sports section of The Times saying, "Bates's fire burning stronger than ever." It actually referred to Ken Bates, then at Leeds United, but could equally well have applied to our own gaffer. He made our team loyal, enjoyable and successful, over 13 long seasons. And his son, Joe, returned from Canada to play in our last 2 seasons, as we won 2 League Titles, 2 League Cups, and lost narrowly in the Middlesex County Cup Final. It was emotional at our last ever end-of-season awards night, a real end-of-an-era occasion. Steven and I had been a bit like Brian Clough and Peter Taylor for those 13 long years, weathering a lot of storms together, and enjoying the roller coaster of a ride.

Steven sorted out his personal life, via a new and stable relationship, plus the arrival of two new (football-playing) daughters. And he expanded his role, initially coaching NPL adults' 1st XI, and more recently with roles at Hampton & Richmond Borough FC: Head of Youth Development, Academy Manager and Assistant Manager of the first team.

Playing an assistant role to Steven was never going to be an easy task, but one or two did try. Martin joined us, as a keen and spirited Assistant Manager. But he was known as 'BBC' by Steven (for bibs, balls and cones), and earned the nickname "Page 19" for his love of a coaching manual. Poor Martin: whenever he tried to follow Steven's full-on and impassioned team talks with some words of wisdom of his own, the boys just wandered off and didn't listen.

But Simon, another dad, performed infinitely better. He was a great foil to Steven, and would step in if the gaffer was away on a coaching course. Simon was as calm, assured and disciplined as Steven wasn't – and his teams would perform in similar mode. If dogs adopt the personality of their owners, perhaps the same is true of football teams?

Simon's training sessions were always ultra-disciplined too, earning him the nickname 'Sergeant-Major'. And the Sergeant-Major was a stickler for officiating and running the line too. Simon would brandish his flag (like a Premier League linesman) whenever a substitute was being made. In one game, Simon flagged an offside, and the opposition captain was outraged. The referee felt the need to stop the game, and have a chat with our firm but fair official. And, like the true professional that he was and is, Simon kept his flag raised throughout their entire minute-long conversation. Surely there has been no finer linesman plying their trade in youth football over recent years?!

CHAPTER 6

PLAYERS & PERSONALITIES

"The strength of the team is each individual member. The strength of each member is the team."
– Phil Jackson.

It takes all sorts of different players and personalities to build a kids' football team - from thoroughbreds to scrappers to the disinterested. (One boy could never remember what the score was; I think he was only there under parental pressure!) To that age-old conundrum, of whether you pick a team to win matches or rotate players to give everyone equal pitch time, Steven would always say, "Give me 18 players of equal ability, and I'll give them all equal pitch time." But of course, players don't come in equal shapes or sizes or abilities, any more than they come in equal personalities. And thank goodness for that - because we had some great and glorious individuals play for us over the years... and this chapter is dedicated to them. Warts and all!

⚽

Let's start with the goalkeepers - always a thankless task. I'm still baffled why Premier League strikers are so revered and command multi-million-pound transfer fees way in excess of goalkeepers, and yet a goal saved is every bit as valuable as a goal scored. It also seems grossly unfair that one mistake by a keeper is seen to cost his team the game, when a striker can miss two absolute sitters, but as long as he scores the third, he's still lauded as a hero.

The first Hampton Rangers goalie was Oli. He was vocal, but in a very high-pitched voice; he was, after all, only 7 or 8! But the instructions to his defence would echo shrilly around Hatherop Park. One parent dryly remarked, "It sounds like he's ordering a Chinese takeaway!" Big Norman, Oli's dad, was as a taciturn as Oli was vocal: he would prowl around behind the goal, like a male lion, ready to pounce. Oli went on, I believe, to become an international canoeist for Great Britain. Must have been all those prawn crackers!

Next came Felix, sharing his name with the great Brazilian goalkeeper from 1970. And with a name like Felix, surely he would become "The Cat"? But while Felix was a great shot-stopper, the similarities ended there. He was a happy and smiley kid, and someone who always wanted to clown around (don't all goalies?) and was desperate to play out of goal (aren't all goalies?) It wasn't until the later years that we managed to sign a 'proper' goalkeeper, Max Ward - someone who really wanted to play in goal - and his presence and ability vastly improved the whole team.

With NPL, the keeper progression was not dissimilar. Initially different boys took it in turns. It always seemed like fun to be in goal, diving around with big gloves on. But the fun quickly dissipated as the goals went in. Sam Cheah always liked to don the gloves - but he was far too good and valuable a player out on-pitch to be 'wasted' in goal.

So we signed someone we thought was a new keeper, James Meadows, to ensure we had a permanent presence between the sticks. He came as a 'job lot', with two other rugby boys, Alex Cozens and Tom Tosetti. But we soon realised James wasn't a keeper, just an all-round talented athlete. He moved out of goal, and would storm all over the pitch. Steven once said he needed to tie James to a post in the middle of the park (like a goat), to ensure he kept some shape and tactical discipline. James went on to play professional rugby league, and is currently earning a living as a stand-off, scrum-half or fullback for the London Broncos. He too was always going to be 'wasted' in goal.

Finally, as with Wardy at Rangers, we found a 'proper' keeper to transform the team. And it was another Max too, this one called Max Bramhall. His father, Big Adam, had been a goalkeeper in his youth, so he always advocated the role, saying it was the one position you'd always be guaranteed a game, and never get substituted. Young Max was brought up with that mindset – and what a keeper he turned out to be.

When we first signed Max, Big Adam brought him to watch an away game at Epsom Eagles, before his registration card had come through. I knew from that moment that we'd signed a 'team player' – and a great 'team family' too, along with his mum Maria and his sister Georgia. Indeed, they all stayed with us for over 10 years. Big Adam's cheer-leading was based around his self-styled slogan, "You'll Never Beat The Bramhall" – and he had a personalised T-shirt made to promote the message. Such was the success of said T-shirt, that a new one emerged the following season, "Jesus Saves… but not as many as The Bramhall"!

The match reports record our relief on finally finding a decent goalie: "After 4 long seasons, maybe we have finally now found a proper keeper who actually wants to play in goal!"

And a few years later, "With his new Paul Robinson haircut, Max pulled off some brave and spectacular saves, with the terrace chant going up: 'You'll Never Beat The Bramhall...' Unfortunately, they did (with a fine headed goal from a corner) and we lost the game 1-0!"

There is also reference to a fine away win at Carshalton Athletic: "Word reached me during the week that it's been 25 years (and about 13 stone) since a Bramhall was last in goal on the Westminster City School pitches. The chip-off-the-old-block saved us twice during the second half today, with a brave collision stop and a one-on-one saved with his legs – and he also tested the Manager's dodgy heart by nearly dropping a ball over the line." But all keepers need a bit of self-belief and cockiness, don't they? "Max clawed one back off the line in the first half (more 'Panther' than 'Cat') and made an excellent one-on-one save after the break. He then said he got up to find something in his back pocket – their centre forward!"

There are fewer written records of the Hampton Rangers days and players. But we did reach some Cup Finals, and the player profiles from the programmes help to summarise the personalities. So here's an introduction and compilation of some of those who wore the red and yellow of Hampton Rangers over the years – the good, the bad and the ugly!

FELIX CHOW – reliable shot-stopper who, despite his occasional reluctance to play in goal, attracted interest from Valencia on last year's tour.

MAX WARD – voluble goalkeeper who joined Rangers as one of 6 new summer signings. Good kicking and always liable to stop the un-stoppable.

BEN NAUGHTON-RUMBO – full back and former Player of the Year, who has stepped up a gear this year to make the right back position his own.

JOE PATTEN – progressed through the Colts to become a colossus at the back. His never-say-die attitude has made him a frequent former Player of the Year.

JACK CHRISTOPHERS – two-footed ball-playing centre back, now in his 9th season with Rangers. Voted Player of the Year last season.

MATT PURSEY – joined Rangers in the summer, and has rapidly established himself as a footballing centre back, who loves to get forward as well.

CAINE MARSHALL – another summer signing whose no compromise displays at left back are reminiscent of Stuart "Psycho" Pearce.

STUART MCLAREN – one-time goalkeeper, but now a tough-tackling full back who has come through a series of injuries to reclaim his place.

ALEX RAMSAY – club captain who leads by example. A ball-winning defensive midfielder who covers every blade of grass, week in, week out.

BROOK DRIVER – diminutive midfielder with massive energy and a massive heart: he never stops running. Great leader, both on and off the pitch.

FRED PARKER – a strong, tall central midfielder, in his first season with Rangers. Can also fill in at the back if required.

HENRY LANGFORD – much-talking midfielder who likes to

attack; off-the-field he recorded the club's official anthem *We Will Rock You.*

TRISTAN LOFFLER – pacy winger or attacking midfielder who never gives up, and has now begun to score goals as well.

SIMON VEASEY – midfielder or defender who has Hampton Rangers in his blood: the third Veasey son to play for Rangers, and his dad's also been Manager.

VISHAL MAKOL – skilful midfielder with great technique. Has grown in strength and confidence, and is now getting in amongst the goals.

JOE BARWICK – speedy winger who joined Rangers in the January transfer window 2006, so now in his first full season.

ED HIGGINS – has led the line for Rangers for the last few seasons as top goal scorer. Skillful striker who holds the ball up well.

SAMUCA COKER – a former Player of the Year who's now in his second spell with Rangers. Electric pace, great technique and a massive heart.

ANDREA CAIO – new continental signing from Italy with great touch and skill. A striker with real vision, who can also deputise in goal if needed.

BOBBY KHANGURRA – striker or winger in his first season with the club; played as the lone striker in the semi-final win.

ASH AMHAMA – new signing who can play at the back or in midfield, bringing ball-winning commitment to the team.

DAN HUGHES – pacy striker or winger with a combative attitude; now in his second season at the club.

CALUM MANSON – tricky winger with a sweet left foot who has played for Rangers for several years.

NAT JOWITT – one-time super-sub who's now developed into an accomplished full back.

ANDY MCLAREN – Goalkeeping Coach and part-time Referee whose commitment and enthusiasm have benefitted Rangers over recent years.

EDUARDO RUBIO – the Spanish José Mourinho, now in his third season as Coach. An inspiration to the team and parents alike.

STEVEN HIGGINS – Team Manager whose hours on the training ground and organisational skills have helped to improve Rangers over the past 3 seasons.

DENIS CHAPLIN – President and Club Treasurer who has worked tirelessly for Rangers for over 35 years, and is still desperately seeking some silverware…

That's quite a comprehensive list of the Hampton Rangers players and management from the 2006-2007 era. But there are also one or two notable omissions. Big Ben (to distinguish him from Little Ben) came down from Yorkshire to join the team, a few years earlier. He arrived with his father, Big Roger (the adjective clearly runs in the family). Big Roger told us, with supreme confidence and self-belief, that we only had to put the ball in the box, and Big Ben would put it in the back of the net. But Big Ben wasn't quite as bullish as his old man. Three seasons later, we were still waiting for him to open his account!

⚽

There's on old Swedish proverb that says the much-loved child has many names. And by the time NPL were reaching Cup Finals, the player profiles begin to reflect this, with the advent of nicknames. It's probably a function both of a more relaxed approach to match reporting (it's much harder to take the mickey out of an 8-year-old than an 18-year-old), and also of Big Adam's observational humour. So, here's an introduction to some of NPL's very finest, taken from the 2015-2017 years.

MAX "YOU'LL NEVER BEAT THE" BRAMHALL - part of a goalkeeping dynasty, and pulls off a customary 1 or 2 world class saves every match; never short of an opinion or three.

LIAM "RIGHT BACK IN THE CHANGING ROOM" HEATH - dogged Tottenham terrier of a full back who always takes the man, and sometimes the ball as well; liable to score one goal every 10 years.

WILL "CALMNESS" CHRISTOPHERS - our calm and composed captain: intelligent distribution, strong aerial presence and bright boots too; also our penalty king.

WILL "THE ROCK" WESTLAND - our Mr Dependable, who breaks up attacks time after time; trying hard to shrug off his "sick note" title.

ALEX "MILLWALL" PEARSON - new summer signing who has been the Stuart Pearce 'Psycho' of the team; never misses a game, a training session or a physical challenge.

RYAN "MK DONS" DAVID - a footballing thoroughbred who has brought class and composure to the back line; fantastic team player, willing to prioritise club over county.

MASON "DURACELL" WORSFOLD-GREGG - the Road Runner of the team, who never stops: tenacious, athletic and versatile; has played in every position for the team, including in goal.

THEO "THE GAZELLE" OSBORNE – pace, precision, assists and even goals: with a bit more self-belief, could become our Gareth Bale.

LUKE "SQUEAKY" BROOKER – part of the original NPL team; a fine utility player with great mindset, pace and athleticism; wears what Big Adam informs me is a "high & tight" footballers' haircut.

ALEX "RIVERDANCE" SEALY – deceptively effective as a second-half impact sub, rarely misses a tackle, and shows real pace and power too.

JOSH "THE SNOOD" THOMPSON – sponsored by Claire's Accessories, a left back with fine flowing locks, and a laconic brand of sarcasm too.

KAILAN "HAPPY" NORTH – unquenchable energy and running ability; immense heart and determination, in the engine room or wide right; nice tights, and even the odd smile.

ALEX "HOUSE ELF" BROWN – baby-faced assassin, who keeps the ball moving, never wastes possession, and plays the game with a smile on his face: the sort of player Cloughie would have loved.

DEAN "THE DESTROYER" BYNE – holding midfield general, neat and tidy in possession; Watford Academy's loss has been NPL's gain; everyone needs a nutter in the middle!

HENRY "SLO-MO" NEWTON-SAVAGE – great touches of skill and game understanding, scoring some vital goals; an original NPL-er; rather unkindly called "Cement Boots"!

JOSH "BITES YOUR LEGS" BLACKMAN – combative and fearless midfielder who breaks up play for fun, in a Roy Keane-esque sort of way. Fuelled by Vodka Red Bull.

CHRIS "SICK NOTE" WORT – a true thoroughbred of a footballer, whose class and creativity can turn a game in an instant; play-maker with guile and Don Juan good looks too.

JOE "CHIP OFF THE OLD BLOCK" BATES – welcomed back from Canadian exile as a robust and skilful midfielder-come-No 10, with a keen eye for goal (and for the girls too).

SAM "CHEETAH" CHEAH – our game breaker and game changer, with Usain Bolt-like pace; goals plus numerous assists from the (these days) not-so-little master.

ALFIE "GOAL MACHINE" POPE – an Alan Shearer of a striker, who rampages through the middle, scoring with right, left or head; our very own Roy of The Rovers, with zero ego or arrogance.

CHARLIE "100%" HOLMES – pacey striker with a great work ethic and a proper footballer's haircut; never gives less than everything, never gives up, and never without new boots.

KAI "SWEET LEFT FOOT" HANLEY – delivers a cross as good as any Premier League winger, weighing in with important goals too. Also possesses a key sense of sarcasm.

ABS "MAGIC FEET" RAJAB – a self-proclaimed street footballer, who adds pace, trickery and unpredictability to the NPL attack; also has one of the biggest smiles in youth football.

WILL "THE TANK" DAVEY – solid and determined winger, who lets his feet do the talking; impossible to shake off the ball, and can be a dark horse of a match winner.

Also **CALLUM "THE GHOST" CASTLING, CHARLIE "QUICK FEET" PIKE, JACK "THE ROCK" SMITH**, and twin brothers **BEN & LEWIS GALLIFENT** (Charlton and Neville brothers, eat your hearts out).

STEVEN "THE GUV'NOR" BATES – charismatic, colourful, controversial, and one of youth football's most passionate. Coach and manager who wears his heart on his sleeve; renowned for his motivational team talks, tactical nous and infectious enthusiasm.

⚽

There were many others too – I recall 2 x Luca's, 2 x Alfie's, 2 x Sam's and an unprecedented 5 x Alex's. But several of the early years NPL-ers also warrant mention. 8-year-old Tom was a defender who always reminded me of one of those toy football figures, whose head you press down for them to kick the ball, with a straight foot (no bend in the knee) to a 90-degree angle. His father Stuart helped with the coaching, and Tom had the stoicism if not the athletic ability of his old man. But he could time a tackle, and would frequently win the ball with Bobby Moore-style precision, when faced with 2 or 3 oncoming attackers.

Jake was another who was brought along by his football-coaching dad, Barry. Barry was as vocal and full-on as Jake wasn't, and used to shout "Hunt it down, Jake" whenever the opposition goalkeeper had the ball. I had visions of a perplexed-looking Jake, in a hunting hat, not quite sure what he was actually meant to be hunting down.

There's probably another chapter to be written on fathers, sons and football. So many of us are desperate for our sons to play and enjoy the beautiful game, and even to excel at it.

But not all sons share their father's enthusiasm or even their ability, which can cause a lot of friction and heartache, both ways round.

One Hampton Rangers boy had a father who was desperate for him to play and to succeed. The dad used to run down the touchline whenever his boy had the ball, urging him forward, and living vicariously through his reluctant son. The manager, Denis, used to say that this boy was a much better and more confident footballer when his father wasn't there – and I noticed how the poor lad would almost shrink into his shirt and try to render himself invisible, whenever his father was watching. He grew up to excel in many other avenues in life – but football was never going to be one of them.

At NPL, Ted was a fragile and timid striker, who was always much more interested in classic cars than football – as was his father! But it worked in other ways as well. Theo's father, Andrew, had been a keen and talented footballer himself, but his own father had never taken much interest in his game. So Andrew never missed one of Theo's matches, and was always there to encourage and support him. Theo had great athleticism, as an overlapping left back, and Steven would always shout "Travel" when he got the ball in space. He grew up to become a male model – so he travelled far from that left back position! And Keith's support for his pocket-rocket of a footballing son, Sam, was such that he saw red when Sam didn't get what his dad deemed to be sufficient pitch-time minutes. The tightrope of managing tensions, expectations and egos in kids' football…

⚽

Sam Cheah was a mainstay of the NPL team, especially during the early years. His father, Kim, the self-styled 12th Man of the

NPL team, was born in Malaysia as the youngest of 10 siblings – so he was always put in goal. And Sam's mother, Karen, was a sprinter for Wales – so she gifted Sam his blistering pace. Sam was one of 5 players from that original NPL Class of 2004 (in the team when they were just 5 years old) who was still playing 13 years later; the others being Will, Joe, Alex Brown and Mason.

But Sam was a multi-talented sportsman, who was keen to turn his hand to rugby, and also developed a real skill for athletics, and triple jumping in particular. So we had to use a lot of persuasion and ingenuity to keep the mercurial Welsh-Malaysian on side. Here's a contract that was duly prepared; who knows if something similar would have kept Harry Kane at Tottenham Hotspur?

I, Samuel Willem Gwilliam Cheah, do hereby solemnly commit my sporting future to NPL Youth Football Club.

I apologise unreservedly for even thinking about playing rugby next season, and I admit this was a rash and ill-advised sentiment, for which I can only blame the 12th Man.

I concede that while becoming the first Triple-Jumping Footballer to represent Great Britain at the Olympics is a strong possibility, the prospect of becoming a Triple-Jumping Rugby-playing athlete is just plain ridiculous.

I understand that the beautiful game is played with a round ball, and that it was an error of judgement for me to ever think otherwise.

I freely admit that the afore-mentioned 12th Man has contributed little to my sporting genes, and that these come primarily from my maternal Welsh ancestry, Ruabon's Wrexham Express.

I fully understand that any failure by me in signing this contract will lead to the irrevocable and immediate release of the N-Dubz video, and that my dance moves will therefore be guaranteed to go viral.

⚽

Kailan was like The Tasmanian Devil cartoon character, a whirlwind of energy and athleticism. He reminded me of Roy Keane in his glory days (and he could be just as grumpy too) of whom Sir Alex Ferguson said, "If I was putting Roy Keane out there to represent Manchester United on a one-against-one, we'd win the Derby, the National, the Boat Race and anything else." Kailan was more graft and combat than finesse, but he still fancied himself for a free kick - backed by his father too. History records, "Up stepped Kailan… Tony's words were still echoing in my ears… '9 times out of 10, Kailan puts the ball into the top corner from that range…' It wasn't Row Z, but maybe Row K?! Never mind, I'm sure he'll find the net with the next 9!"

We had plenty of good people over the years, and some great personalities too. Abs, previously referenced as a self-proclaimed street footballer, was able to skip over the mud and marauding opposition challenges. Diminutive in size but strong and powerful on the ball, he brought to mind that old ad slogan, *"Weebles wobble, but they don't fall down!"* Dean was the definition of efficiency on the ball, Mr "Neat & Tidy" - although his dad said that's not how his bedroom looks! And Kai could pick a pinpoint cross with his wand of a left foot - "a better delivery than DHL", as the manager used to say.

Ryan was a towering and assured presence at centre back, who loved going up for a header with the rallying cry, "Ryan's Up!" We even once signed a player called Darcy - and I don't think that's a name widely in use across

Sunday morning kids' football pitches. But it did enable the touchline cry, whenever he got the ball, of "Pass, Darce!"

And then there was the boss's prodigal son, Joe, who came back to play for NPL again after 6 long years in exile, in the land of ice hockey in Canada. But fortunately, his footballing genes were strong – and he never lost his eye for goal.

CHAPTER 7

THE 12TH MAN

"Football is nothing without fans." – Sir Matt Busby.

Just like every football club, the fanbase is very much part of the extended team. And over the years we were blessed with some outstanding off-field support – from parents, to grandparents, siblings, friends, uncles and aunts. We frequently had 20-30 people coming to support our boys, whether at home or travelling away. As the boys grew older, we referred to some of the supporters as MAGs, instead of WAGs (mums and girlfriends, as opposed to wives and girlfriends). At times, the MAGs would be out in force, conspicuous away in Hanworth in their fur-lined hoods and boots!

The old African proverb says that it takes a whole village to raise a child – and you certainly also need a whole team of willing helpers to raise a kids' football team. Volunteer linesmen, match reporters, end-of-season tour planners, team photographers, goalkeeping coaches, sponsors and kit suppliers; there are always plenty of jobs to get stuck into.

There was some great parental support through the Hampton Rangers days, notably from the Veasey family (a footballing dynasty, with 3 sons all playing for the club) and latterly with the aforementioned Big Roger (who makes me wonder whether every kids' team needs at least one "Big" parent?)

The Pope family at NPL were great supporters. Alfie, our free-scoring No 9, enabled us to write headlines such as "Alfie 4 Pope", when he scored 4 times in a game. Keith, his dad, was always visible on the touchline – small in size, but often in an unmissable high-vis jacket. Alfie's little brother Ted would often come along, wearing a replica NPL kit, while Tracey, his mum, was famed for her post-match Sunday lunches. Whenever Alfie scored a hat-trick, there were extra roast potatoes and pork crackling!

Keith often watched the matches with Graham, who was as tall as Keith was short. So they soon became known as Del Boy and Rodney, an impressive double act on the touchline – "No income tax, no VAT" – or occasionally the Morecambe and Wise of Sunday League football – "Bring me sunshine!" One year, when we clinched a league title, Graham was tasked with sprinting off (when the final whistle blew) to fetch the chilled champagne. He surged too early, and slipped down a grassy bank, all 6-feet-7 of him going 'arse over tit' down the hill. More Trigger than Eric Morecambe, that particular Sunday morning.

Kim Cheah has already been mentioned as the self-styled NPL 12th Man, and his wife Karen was also often on the touchline, even forming the mums' group of "Cheah Leaders". Kim's constant touchline cry was "Pass-the-ball-to-Sam-Cheah", which could be heard ringing around the touchlines of the Surrey Youth League on a Sunday morning. He would always lead the line in driving to away matches, with supreme belief in his own in-head sat nav.

Kim also liked to weigh in with the odd bit of tactical advice – although he was nowhere to be seen at training on a cold Wednesday night. While NPL were famed for playing bright, sharp, attacking football, Kim could be heard from the touchline shouting, "Hoof it!" Kim became the self-appointed specialist heading coach, waxing lyrical about a heading masterclass he once ran in a caravan on our Isle of Wight tour. Kim never took himself too seriously, and his NPL legacy is neatly summed up in this incident: "So, with the game dead-locked at 1-1, it was left to Kim Cheah to shout 'keeper's ball' as a Horsley free kick flew towards our goal... Our defence took Kim's word for it, left it, and Horsley duly scored the winner!"

Quentin was always a laconic presence on the touchline. He came as part of a package deal, when his son and 2 other boys joined from Roehampton Rangers. Quentin was always willing to volunteer, in a coaching or linesman capacity, and would fulfill these roles with trademark wit and sarcasm. Records from one game note, "With our superiority beginning to show, they shocked us again on the stroke of half-time, with a breakthrough goal that was ruled on-side – by linesman Quentin, resplendent in his Alan Partridge sports casual corduroys... So who were we to disagree?"

As the boys grew up, so the touchline girlfriends began to appear. Our keeper Max brought Sophie along, boldly proclaiming to anyone who would listen, "She's the one". He then proceeded to make every simple save look difficult, in moves which became known as the Max Factor. Nando's dates and the lure of Peri-Peri chicken began to compete with midweek training commitments.

⚽

The end-of-season Dads' Tournaments were always a source of great entertainment, both on and off the pitch. Kim "The Cat" Cheah would play in goal, until he was replaced by

Adam "The Octopus" Bramhall. Wearing one of his trademark T-shirts, with "Max's Dad, No 1" on the back, Big Adam was surprisingly nimble for a big fellow, and single-handedly saved us in most of our games.

Hakim lived up to his name, as did Mr T from the A-Team, always taking the man, quite oblivious to any ball. Alex "Flat-on-his-Backside" Tosetti would put in a useful shift, even occasionally staying upright. Martin "Page 19" Upson proved that he really had played some football in his time – even getting into a bit of handbags to prove the point! And Steve "The Sponsor" Holmes got so powered up on PowerAde that he managed to spill all the kids' chips in his post-goal celebrations, before rupturing his calf.

But he wasn't the only casualty. I'm ashamed to report that we left 2 opposition dads on crutches in 2 consecutive seasons, such was our competitive dad presence. Neil "Chopper" Meadows proved to be more "attacker" than "attacking midfielder", while Barry "The Bruiser" Ruse wasn't taking any nonsense from anyone. Thank goodness these guys were on our side!

Meanwhile Steven "The Guv'nor" Bates would stroll back into his Jan Molby role with consummate ease, showing flashes of his former genius – though he was mobbed by his U10 team when he missed the target for the 15th successive time: "Goals don't move, Steven…"

The end-of-season awards night was also always a great gathering of the full supporters' club. The beers and sambucas would flow freely, and one year the NPL Chairman even performed his own party trick, drinking a pint of Guinness while standing on his head. Who said kids' football isn't entertaining?

CHAPTER 8

THE GLORY GAME

"You'll win nothing with kids." – Alan Hansen.

Football can conjure up some magic moments, can't it? I recently watched a documentary about the late, great Sir Bobby Charlton. He was standing in the middle of the Old Trafford pitch, probably 80 years old, reminiscing about his life and his career. And he was just struck by the awe and wonder of it all. *"It's what you dream of, isn't it? I dreamt of being a footballer. My whole family was football mad. It's just magic. Absolute magic."*

As well as the near misses, there were some momentous achievements over the 25 years I stood on the touchline. With Hampton Rangers, Edu took us to two successive Cup Finals. Unfortunately, we lost both of them – but there was a memorable moment in the second one.

Vish was a lovely boy, football mad, and someone who would train his heart out, to try to keep up with his more naturally gifted team mates. His father, Neeraj, kindly sponsored the team, and supplied the kits, so there was no way he could be dropped from the squad. Edu used him sparingly as a substitute, and Vish developed some of the best warm-up routines you have ever seen. He made Premier League players seem ill-prepared.

In the Cup Final, Edu decided to give Vish the last 5 minutes of the first half, and the first 5 minutes of the second half. "Veeeesh", he would scream at him – but the boy had other ideas. With the game locked at 0-0, on came Vish, and he only went and broke the deadlock – with a deft finish to put us 1-0 up. He was promptly subbed back off again – and we lost the match – but the moment was as priceless as it was unscripted.

⚽

With NPL, we won our first trophy, becoming Epsom & Ewell League Champions, at U10 stage. It was a memorable moment and achievement for the boys, who clinched the title with an emphatic 10-0 win. The yellow and blue hairspray came out of the spray cans, and the alcohol-free champagne was flowing freely. The innocence of youth!

We went on to win a League and Cup Double in each of our last 2 NPL seasons – Surrey Youth Premier Elite Champions and Surrey Youth League Cup Winners – celebrated by special edition "Double Double" T-Shirts. And we were a whisker away from the Treble in that last season too, narrowly losing to Wingate & Finchley in the final of the prestigious Middlesex FA County Cup.

There's a lovely Bobby Robson interview with Gary Lineker, 10 years after Italia 90, and the heartache of a World Cup semi-final penalty shootout defeat to Germany. Bobby says, "We were a whisker away, son. A whisker away." He always liked repeating himself. But we, too, were a whisker away from that unprecedented U18 Treble. Part of "all those oh-so-nears", as documented in the *Three Lions* song, *It's Coming Home*.

But it was our first Surrey Youth Cup Final win that still lives large in the memory. It was billed as the battle of the

Champions: Premier Elite league winners Abbey Rangers (an U18 team) against Premier League winners NPL Youth (we were still an U17 side, the young pretenders). Watching from the stands, I was feeling quite emotional (nothing new there) – I had seen several of our boys play for NPL since they were 5 or 6 years old, and here they were, pulling the strings and playing some fantastic football in an U18 Cup Final.

We were locked at 1-1, against a stronger, fitter and more physical side. Extra time was beckoning; could we hang on? Quentin was reminding the referee that his "2 minutes to go" had already lasted 5 minutes. Luckily, Quentin was ignored. Because in the 98th minute (in a moment that would go down in NPL folklore) Kai sent in one of those teasing, inviting crosses that he did so effortlessly… and there was Alfie on the end of it, to prod the ball home! 2-1 to the NPL, the stadium erupted, and the NPL subs all charged onto the pitch to celebrate. A 98th minute stoppage time winner – what a way to win the Cup! The NPL support was magnificent, as it was across all those years, with Alfie's dad, Keith, leading the celebrations from Majorca, where he had been watching the match on FaceTime!

Some other random but memorable highs are captured in the match reports – the context may have faded from memory, but the emotions remain very much alive!

- "With 5 minutes left, we're under more pressure at the back, but manage to clear the ball… Ellis finds Alex C, who plays a wonderful through ball… the defenders hesitate, but Alex G gallops onto it… the linesman's flag stays down… he's one-on-one with their keeper… and SCORES… it's his first goal for the club… and it's 2-1 to NPL!"

- "And then an iconic and defining moment of the season – the goal-scorer dives flat onto the ground, and is engulfed in the sunshine by 15 blue-shirted teammates. That's what it means to them – and that's what it means to us, too. Great work, great result and great team spirit. A lot of we old men and women are feeling proper chuffed!"

- "3 minutes to go, and up steps Mason. A surging run from left back, jinking past two defenders and lashing the ball across goal. Charlie somehow just gets on the end of it, sending everybody the wrong way. Time stands still as it trickles over the line – unbeaten record in doubt? What was I talking about! Joy and relief on the touchline, and then the final whistle. Football is just brilliant."

- "So 3-1 to Epsom at half-time, and (coming on top of Newcastle's impending relegation) I'm left wondering what to hang on the Toon coat hangers Big Adam has just given me; myself maybe?! But Steven used all his experience during the half-time interval, to get into the head of the referee first, and then of his own side. The hair drier was on full volume, as he questioned our boys' desire and self-belief – and encouraged them to embrace their destiny, and go out to win the league in the second half. I don't know if he expected us to win the second half 5-0, but that's exactly what we went and did…"

- "Cometh the hour, cometh the manager's son. Sent on with instructions to "get us a goal, then get off", he did both – glancing in a fine header from Kai's cross, right into the top corner: 4-3 to NPL."

- "Our 2 subs are long since used, and Liam 'Psycho' Heath is cramping up. 30 minutes of extra time are beckoning. We know there'll only be one winner then – and it won't be us.

Hanging on, and we're into added time. Then something miraculous happens. Alfie 'The Goal Machine' Pope turns provider – or was it Charlie? – I honestly can't remember. But from somewhere, a haunting cross comes over from the left. And there is Kailan, stealing in unmarked at the back post. He's never scored a header in his life. BUT HE DOES NOW! It's 2-1 to NPL, and the final whistle blows immediately."

And what about penalties? A curse or a blessing? Of course, it all depends on the result…

- "It's a long time since we've had a penalty shoot-out – but there's something familiar and reassuring about the captain stepping up to take the first penalty – just as Alan Shearer used to do at Newcastle. And are penalties a lottery? Well maybe not, when you've got a secret weapon called Max in goal. It went something like this… Will scores. Max saves. Kailan scores. Max saves. Jack scores. Inter Ditton score. Alfie scores. Game over: 4-1 to NPL on penalties!"

As Alan Shearer said on his Euro 2024 commentary, while England were defeating Switzerland in the quarter finals with a set of perfect penalties, "Pressure, what pressure? Pressure is for tyres!"

⚽

But I can't conclude a chapter called The Glory Game without a few lines about the unsung heroes. There is an inordinate amount of behind-the-scenes work that goes into running a kids' football team. It's one thing to turn up and support on a Sunday morning, but spare a thought for those who have arrived early, to shovel up the dog and fox shit, fill in the rabbit holes, and put up the nets. Pre-match rituals could involve brooms, sponges, spikes and sand. And even before that, there are pitch inspections to be made, and ringing round parents with postponement or other details; thank goodness for text messaging and WhatApp groups these days.

Then there is the fund raising. At Hampton Rangers, that meant producing mugs, calendars, mouse mats and other merchandise, featuring our players. Also holding race and quiz nights, raffles (with Roger the Raffle invariably in charge), and disco evenings (when John and Debbie Ramsay would show us all how to rock & roll). We would attract between 60 and 100 people at these social nights – and packing bags at Sainsbury's at Christmas was also a lucrative initiative.

Finally, a word for our sponsors. Over the years, we were "proud to be sponsored" by Pacific International Recruitment; NAP Construction Ltd; HKH Building Services Ltd; and Wettons Cleaning Services ("an independent family company with a difference, established 1949"). The last two on this list were the companies of Steven and Nicola Holmes, who were most generous in supporting NPL over several years. There were times when we needed HKH Building Services umbrellas and a sponsored gazebo with outdoor heating. But we carried HKH or Wettons sponsorship on our tracksuits, rain jackets and team shirts (which included a striking AC Milan-style red and black striped away kit; who needs the San Siro?) Big kudos and thanks to all those who helped enable so many kids to play and enjoy their football.

CHAPTER 9

HEARTACHE & PAIN

"It doesn't matter if you win or lose… until you lose."
– Snoopy, in Charlie Brown.

I recently bumped into Steven Bates in Bushy Park. He was telling me about a coaching course he'd attended, and how everyone had to share the worst decision they'd ever witnessed in football. He didn't hesitate. It may have been 16 long years ago, but he was still feeling the injustice of a penalty shoot-out defeat for our U8's team! And I could also still feel the pain.

It was 10th March 2007, and an U8's Cup Semi Final away at Wolves in Guildford. The match report headline captures the emotions, "Crying Shame". Italia 1990, Euros 1996, Lisbon 2004, Gelsenkirchen 2006, The Belmont Bathrooms Cup 2007 - it doesn't get any easier to take. NPL dominated this cup tie from the start. For the first 10 minutes, Wolves never even got out of their own half. It was siege mentality. But, as the old adage goes, you have to score when you're on top - and we just couldn't. Wolves' response was cynical: diving, play acting, shirt-tugging and kicking. It was sad to see an U8 team play with such deceptive tactics: these were sly and cunning Wolves, with little regard for the beautiful game.

In the last minute of the match, a blatant "Hand of God" clearance off the line by their defender (seen by everyone except the referee) denied us either a goal or a penalty. Where's VAR when you need it? So, into extra time we went. It's still 0-0 after extra time, so it's now on to penalties – harsh for anyone, especially 7-year-olds. We lost 3-2 on penalties, and that's when the wheels fell off, and the tears started.

The wounds are still raw, all these years on. But there was revenge of sorts, 7 years later. Wolves were drawn in a Cup tie at NPL, entering the lions' den. We tore our bewildered visitors apart, leaving them in no doubt about our motivation, born from that lingering sense of injustice. They didn't quite know what had hit them, nor why.

"We simply curse, go home, worry for a fortnight, and then come back to suffer all over again." – Nick Hornby in *Fever Pitch.*

Whenever I got a wrong answer at school, after some smart kid had got something right, my German teacher used to ask me a rhetorical question. "What comes after the Lord Mayor's show? Yes, the muck cart, Christophers, the muck cart!" On the touchline, we too had several "muck cart" moments over the years. A fine, gladiatorial win one week, then a disappointing, dispiriting defeat the next.

Lifted from the archives, here are some random highlights – or should I say, spectacular lowlights?

- Leatherhead Predators 6 - 2 NPL Youth. As Stacey Solomon (from Dagenham) sung on the X-Factor the other week, "Nobody said it was easy…" And this Premier League is anything but.

- Well, that was a kick in the teeth, wasn't it? 3-0 up and cruising, and we somehow manage to snatch defeat out of the jaws of victory. Theme of the weekend really, after England let Wales come back to beat them – and Newcastle surrendered a 2-goal lead to Chelsea too. Funny old game… and reminds me of a Paul Gascoigne quote, "I never predict anything, and I never will!"

- The little magician (Abs) exploded through the Sutton defence and slotted home to put us 3-2 ahead! Pandemonium broke out in the stands. NPL were ahead. The league title would be ours. And then the Sutton b******s scored two late goals to win it 4-3! Football, bloody hell...

- Another of Jack's long-throws caused more havoc in the box – and cometh the hour, cometh the Bates, as Joe turns in "the winner": 4-3 to NPL… But no! A late, stray, after-thought of an offside flag, and (after consultation) the referee disallows the "goal"… Alex Pearson's nan was livid, swearing she'd "duff up" the linesman – we might have a Millwall-style riot on our hands!

⚽

While I'm a glass half-full type of guy, it has to be said that there can be humour in the bad times too. One report records that after six consecutive league defeats, we had conceded 23 goals and scored just 3. The match reporter duly disappeared for depression therapy to Loughborough on a Boys' Weekend.

And then, one end-of-season weekday evening, AFC Ewell came to play at NPL. The final result read: NPL Youth 0 – 10 AFC Ewell. How do you find the positives when you lose 10-0? "Ewell Not Want to Read This One…"

0-1   Ewell have to pull your Socks Up
0-2   Ewell want to Forget It
0-3   Ewell Never Believe It
0-4   Ewell Probably Blame the Linesman
0-5   Ewell have to get Revenge on Sunday v Alexandra
       United
0-6   Ewell be Welcomed Back with Open Arms, Max
0-7   Ewell at least have a Laugh at the Dads' Tournament
0-8   Ewell be able to get your own back by Shouting at "T"
0-9   Ewell Win Nothing with Kids?
0-10   But Ewell Never Walk Alone…!

Or indeed, how do you find the positives when your team just gives up, half way through? This result was: NPL Youth 1 – 2 Kingstonian Youth Royals. And the match report was titled "Half Hearted…"

It was a bit like
writing a match report
and
then
stopping
half
way
through…

CHAPTER 10

MEN BEHAVING BADLY

"You've got to learn to love the game more than the result."
– Sir Bobby Robson.

But it's not always easy, is it? The passion, the drama, the (perceived) injustice. Like any kids' football team, we had plenty of incidents over the years. Some 'heat of the moment', some entertaining, and some downright embarrassing.

There was a great Surrey Youth League sign put up before a recent NPL Summer Tournament. "Please Remember," it said; "This is not the World Cup. The Players are Children. The Coaches are Volunteers. The Referees are only Human." Meanwhile, the Hampton Rangers philosophy states to this day that youth football is played to be enjoyed, free from negative adult pressure.

I guess it all stems from over-investment. Which leads to too little respect for referees, and too much expectation of our kids. The veteran Premier League manager Sean Dyche, currently at Everton, recently observed, "You don't scream at your kids when they're learning how to read and write – so why do it when they're learning how to play football?"

Officiating kids' football isn't much fun. I never refereed, but I certainly received my fair share of abuse when running the line. The myopia with which we all watch football can sometimes be ridiculous. The assumption can be that every opposition parent is a cheat.

I once got caught up watching the action, guilty of spectating instead of a playing linesman, so completely forgot to flag an offside goal against our team. But it cut both ways. There was another occasion when I was, genuinely, "unsighted" over a goal-line clearance – so couldn't confirm to the referee whether the opposition had scored against us or not. The boys told me later that the ball they "cleared off the line" was so far over, it nearly hit the back of the net!

We came across some great opposing characters too. In one game, we had two goals flagged "offside" by a rather over-zealous linesman, only for the referee to remain strong and correct in over-ruling him both times. By the time we scored the winner, there were so many "I'm no cheat" pleas from the linesman, it became a case of "thou protesteth too much!"

On another occasion, we came across a referee who just loved to be centre-stage. When even the opposition said, "It's not all about you, Richard", he had the audacity (or was it self-belief) to reply, "Yes it is. I'm in charge. So it IS all about me!" Spare a thought for the kids in kids' football, eh? Even Robin Brown, one of our best-behaved parents, was cautioned by this referee for touchline dissent. And the game was then stopped when the ref noticed me taking some photos for my match report; I was instructed to delete the photos before play could continue, as they had been taken without prior permission.

One of the more bizarre moments was when an opposition back four accused Big Adam of "interfering with play", when all he was doing was having a crafty roll-up!

Back in the Hampton Rangers days, we had a parents' meeting, at which many of the mums (in particular) wanted us to take a stand against obsessive swearing. There was a minute in the meeting notes, titled "Foul & Abusive Language". The action was that we should take a stand, at least at home matches, that foul and abusive language would not be tolerated at Hampton Rangers. Suggestions included keeping supporters 5m back from the pitch; posting a sign before matches in the centre circle; writing to the league and to opposing teams in advance of matches; and, if necessary, stopping the game while tempers subside.

Our next home match was against Feltham Youth, and Steven Higgins was tasked with speaking to the opposition about our new policy. He pulled over their manager before kick-off, politely explaining, "We have a no swearing policy at Hampton Rangers, so I hope you can understand and respect that for today's game?" Without a hint of irony, the Feltham manager came straight back at him: "You're f***ing right, Steve, that's a f***ing great move – there's far too much f***ing swearing in kids' football these days!"

One of the most memorable incidents with Hampton Rangers concerned the goalkeeper's father, Brian Ward. Wardy Senior was a sound and solid salt-of-the-earth guy. He ran his own building company, and kindly sponsored the team, who had Ward Builders emblazoned across their shirts.

One particular Sunday morning, Wardy wasn't too happy with some of the referee's decisions, and he started getting into his ear. The game was stopped on a couple of occasions, for the young ref to have a word with Wardy, and ask him to keep his opinions to himself. By the third time, the referee had had enough. "That's it," he said to Wardy, "I'm sending you off." And he brandished a red card. There was a moment's pause, before a perplexed-looking Wardy asked, "But where do I go?" Another pause, as the referee surveyed the scene around Hatherop Park. He soon spotted a large oak tree. "Over there," he said, "You can go and stand behind that tree!" The walk of shame followed. And we couldn't help but notice Wardy peeping round the tree in the second half, trying to catch some of the action.

⚽

There were times when Steven Bates at NPL loved nothing more than a bit of a touchline scrap on a Sunday morning – although for the most part, he kept his emotions in check. But we had an infamous end to our second Surrey Youth League Cup Final win. We were 2-1 up against Roehampton Rangers, and hanging on with the finish in sight, so emotions were beginning to run high. An awful knee-high challenge on one of our young players left him in pieces on the floor. This was too much for most of us - especially with Alfie and Kailan already out on crutches, and Liam having just been carried off with a twisted knee too.

So perhaps it was understandable that Steven let rip at the referee - and achieved a first in his 12 years of coaching this team, namely a red card for himself. Personally, I blame Quentin. His one role in the dugout was to keep Steven calm – and what does he do? He gets our manager sent off! It was all too much for Kailan too, who by this stage had forgotten his injured knee and was wading into the melee on the pitch; (though he claims he thought the final whistle had gone). It did soon after, and we had won the Cup – though the manager had to watch the presentations from a distance.

But Barnes Eagles away was the worst. It was a sad, disappointing and embarrassing low point across all those years. We were warned before the match that the referee was inexperienced and needed our support. Some of his first half decisions clearly frustrated both sets of players. But it was the touchline arguments that flared up mid-way through the second half that really lit the touch paper.

It's difficult to remember how it all started, and then escalated so quickly, but things rapidly descended out of control. Argument, cynicism and dissent had begun on the pitch, but soon spread to the supporters. "Break his legs," one parent shouted. Then another was insulting someone's partner. And before we knew it, one parent (and one of ours, too) had head-butted another parent on the touchline! Unbelievable, but true. A brawl, and chaos, ensued. The poor young referee was left with no alternative but to abandon the match.

Football is a passionate game – that's part of its appeal, and you can't take the emotion away. Moaning about decisions as they happen (or don't) is part of the mix, and we all do it. But discipline and clear boundaries are vital. That day, the behaviour of both sets of parents was unprecedented, indefensible and unacceptable. Luckily, it was the first and only time something like that happened in my 25 years on the touchline.

⚽

It was easier to see the funny side of some parental behaviour. T was the father of Yousef, a small and willowy left-winger, with a deft touch. T was a big and aggressive man (he may have run some big business, I'm not sure). But he was certainly wholly committed to seeing his son succeed on the football field – and he would always station himself on the left wing, to add his comments, encouragement and points of view. After one sublime volleyed goal by Yousef, T celebrated like he'd won the lottery.

But things turned sour on an end-of-season tour to Butlins. Yousef had gone into his shell a little, so he wasn't selected to play in our semi-final match. T was seething at the team selection. So much so, that he began to switch allegiances, and start supporting the opposition. At first, he scowled and loitered behind the goal. But then, he went for a full-on conversion to the other side, joining the opposition parents on the far touchline, away from his own team and his own son. When the tie went to penalties, he made no secret of where his support lay, vocally celebrating all of the opposition goals. We lost that particular penalty shoot-out – and were faced with the image of T running up and down the touchline, celebrating and revelling in our disappointment!

⚽

But sometimes we did OK. In fact, most of the time we did. It was gratifying to see the Surrey Youth Chairman send out a note to all league managers after one top-of-the-table clash, saying, "Today I went to watch NPL v Sutton. All I can say is, what a great advert for youth football. Competitive, fair, 3-0 up to Sutton at half-time, but NPL clawed their way back to 3-2. Everyone enjoyed it and a great referee performance, too." And also, to see the NPL Chairman tweet, "A pleasure to watch a squad play with such confidence… a great showcase of how youth football, at grassroots level, should be played… Passion channeled into the right area, the football… Another positive from the game: all parents, players and officials adhered to the FA Respect campaign." Amen and alleluia to that!

CHAPTER 11

PERMISSION TO DREAM

"Beauty comes first. Victory is secondary. What matters is joy."

So said Socrates - the Brazilian footballer, not the Greek philosopher - though in truth he was a bit of both. Kids' football was always best when it combined beauty and victory - and that certainly constitutes joy!

The beautiful game is, in my opinion, best played with the ball on the ground, played in to feet. The passing game is easy on the eye, though not always easy to execute. The late Johan Cruyff said: *"Playing football is very simple, but playing simple football is the hardest thing there is."*

Steven was a big advocate of this type of football. The NPL philosophy was based around The Steven Bates Academy: getting the ball, keeping the ball and passing the ball. It was great to watch the boys play out from the back with supreme confidence. So when Steven ever said, "Put your laces through it", we knew it was only a temporary measure, designed to adapt to the circumstances!

Pep Guardiola is, of course, today's custodian of beautiful simplicity, but I was brought up in the Brian Clough era. Cloughie would hand his players a football, saying, "This, young man, is your friend - do not give it away." On the importance of passing to feet, he was also famed for saying, "If God had wanted us to play football in the clouds, he'd have put grass up there." It was often a pure joy to watch our boys play football like this on a Sunday morning.

⚽

I never believed any of our kids would become professional footballers - they (and we) were there for the enjoyment, rather than to make a career out of it. One of the boys' older brothers was signed by Chelsea's Academy when he was aged 8. But when they dropped him, aged 12, he fell out of love with football, and never kicked a ball again for the next 5 years, turning to rugby instead. The football pyramid can be harsh and unforgiving.

But one player came dangerously close - and not necessarily the obvious star player type, either. Charlie Holmes was an immensely hard-working and dedicated striker, who would run the channels unselfishly, and run himself into the ground too. He apparently displayed the same tenacity when Dagenham & Redbridge signed him for their Academy, as their new scholar. He even stayed behind to sweep the changing rooms - earning him the title of "sweeper" when he returned to the NPL fold. But jokes aside, "Chazza" became available as a player to sign on FIFA PlayStation - no mean feat (and no mean feet, either) - so unsurprisingly, all his teammates signed him for their teams! Several other boys were also selected by Middlesex FA to play county football - always a blessing in disguise, as we lost them for vital league games.

⚽

We were honoured one Sunday morning when Ray Lewington, at that time Assistant Manager to Roy Hodgson for the England national team, turned up to watch our team. We were trailing 2-0 at half-time, and Ray had a quiet tactical word with Steven, advising that he should push our full-backs much further forward in the second half, and bring our wide front players more central, to create space down the flanks. Surprise, surprise – we ran out 4-2 winners. Perhaps you can teach an old dog new tricks.

At Hampton Rangers, we signed a nippy ginger-haired winger called Joe Barwick, without initially realising that his father was Brian Barwick, then Chief Executive at The Football Association. Brian was a great team man, Liverpool through and through, and he used to love getting away from the pressures of the FA job to watch kids' football. I saw him quoted in one of the tabloids, talking about attending grassroots kids' football on a Sunday morning. He said that some of the things he saw thrilled him, and some things horrified him!

We held a parents' meeting at The Railway Bell, also known as The Dip, in Hampton. And although he was in the midst of appointing a new England manager at the time, Brian insisted he would turn up, to support us all. He was smuggled into the pub, with decoy taxis trying to throw the preying paparazzi off his scent. He phoned his PR, hoping to avoid headlines of "Barwick in pub, when he should be finding new England manager." Anyway, he got away with it – and next morning announced to the press that he was appointing Fabio Capello as the new England manager, to replace Steve McClaren.

We occasionally came across famous footballers from other sides, and Gianfranco Zola always springs to mind. Hampton Rangers were playing away, and Zola's son, Andreas, was playing up front for the opposition. I spotted Zola himself before the match, and went over to say hello. I hadn't realised he was on his phone, so I quickly apologised, and went off to watch the match, thinking nothing more of it. 10 minutes later, he comes all the way round the pitch to find me, and apologises for not talking earlier. We watched the first half together, with my son Jack marking his son Andreas. Neither of them were the quickest, but both were technically gifted. But I'll never forget that gesture from the gent that is Gianfranco.

CHAPTER 12

MATCH REPORTING

"He had it on a plate. He had the sausage, bacon and eggs on it as well, but he couldn't take it." – Chris Kamara.

Football punditry and reporting is a wonderful sub-culture all of its own. I grew up with the poetic sounds of John Moston, Brian Moore and Stuart Hall echoing in my ears. It's a noble art, and there's always a new drama developing or story to be told.

When I look back over 25 years of match reporting, I'm struck by certain recurring soundbites. "We rattled the crossbar… We didn't deserve to be on the losing side… Everyone saw it but the ref… Many positives to take out of this defeat… We were solid at the back… We were back to our best today…"

But you also have to at least try to find the humour – because it's a funny old game, after all, isn't it? Some lines struck me, like kicking off after observing a Remembrance Day silence: "We remained a bit quiet after the 2-minute silence."

Headlines were always a potential source of humour, and a way of summarising all our feelings. A few that spring to mind:

"WET WET WET" – when we lose 6-0 to South Park Juniors in a downpour of a thunderstorm.

"EAGLES STUFFED" – after a 2-1 away win at Epsom Eagles.

"EWELL WIN SOME, EWELL LOSE SOME" – we lose 5-2 away at AFC Ewell.

"LIONS DEVOURED" – following an 8-1 away win at Hearts of Teddlothian Lions.

"OX SHOT TO PIECES" – after winning 5-0 away at Oxshott Royals.

Sometimes the headlines could tell a bit of a story. After a busy January – when we lost a player ("OWAIN GOING") and a manager ("POWER CUT") – we then brought in 3 new rugby players in the transfer window ("NEW BALLS, PLEASE"). Then, playing away at Woking Town, and losing at half-time, I was penning a "CHOKING IN WOKING" report. But a convincing second-half win turned that around, and into: "CHOKING? YOU MUST BE JOKING!"

Clichés, metaphors and analogies are prevalent among the match reporter's armoury, and these were trotted out with ease every week.

- "Jake was like a tigerish Nicky Butt in midfield… Sam Cheah was at his impish menacing best… Alex was solidly reassuring, before heading off quad-biking… And Tom's sharpness up front matched his smart new haircut!"

- "Aside from that, it was a bitterly cold morning, with a hard, semi-frozen pitch, making ball control very difficult. It was bobbly as hell, and that wasn't just Robin Brown's hat on the touchline."

- "Roehampton rattled our post from a superb free kick, with Max stranded. But as Peter Shilton used to say, 'I don't bother stopping the ones that are going to hit the woodwork.' Then came a really classy full-length diving save from our green-clad keeper – moving across the goal like a muddled lime in a mojito…"

The post became the "beans on toast" – enabling such prose as, "Both Alfie and Jack hit the 'beans on toast' when open goals beckoned, and Joe managed arguably the miss of the season, blazing high, wide and handsome at the end, when a simple tap-in would have done!"

And record is made of an 11-0 win, when we also managed to miss a shedload of chances as well. As Big Adam commented at the time, "We couldn't hit a cow's arse with a banjo." That prompted some serious research into the origin of the saying. It's explained as a phrase usually used to describe a sub-standard football player, whose shooting ability leaves a lot to be desired. It's a variation on the classic phrase, "You couldn't hit a barn door from 10 paces." And there may be some Geordie history behind it too. Jackie Milburn says his father used to say, "Son, yer couldn't hit a cow's arse with a shovel." There's a shovel that's called a banjo, because it's shaped like the musical instrument. So there we go!

⚽

What's in a name? When thinking of football club names, I'm always reminded of the beautiful sketch by Ron Manager (aka Paul Whitehouse), as he sits alone in an empty Hartlepool United stadium, talking about Saturday afternoons and football. Even if the end of this clip becomes a little gender-stereotypical, it's still well worth a watch on YouTube, with Whitehouse's nostalgic and compelling delivery.

"Manchester United, Blackburn Rovers, Wolverhampton Wanderers, Sheffield Wednesday, The Arsenal, isn't it? Tottenham Hotspur, Preston North End, Charlton Athletic, Crystal Palace, West Ham United. Mmm? Reassuring names, aren't they? When you're listening, in some far-flung corner of the globe, on the World Service, of a Saturday afternoon... Crackly reception, interference, cosy... Marvellous! Ooh, results; 4:45, Grandstand, isn't it? Highlights on Match of the Day. Somehow comforting, isn't it? You know, legendary names: Tony Gubba. Fathers and sons, on the terraces, cheesy peas at half-time. Pint for dad. Mum's at home, making the tea. Aah! Everything's all right with the world, isn't it? Saturday afternoons. Football. Mmm?"

Kids' football team names can be just as intriguing – if not quite as evocative. What must our opponents have made of our NPL name? The National Physical Laboratory is the place where the bouncing bomb was first invented. NPL today is still the national measurement standards laboratory for the UK, setting and maintaining physical standards for British industry. With a tagline like "Setting standards in analytical science", we must have confused many visiting teams. Surely our football was more art than science?

West Byfleet Scorpions seemed to be the sort of team that could sting you into action in the first minute. Walton Casuals Youth proved to be a scrappy and physically robust Route One side, with nothing Casual about them at all. Their only bright and lively feature was their electric neon shirts.

The poor Mole Valley Predators. We beat them 10-1, with a "MOLES SKINNED" headline – they were anchored to the bottom of the league, Predators in name alone. Brockham Badgers Blues got 10 out of 10 for having an alliteration of a name. But they weren't Badgers, and they didn't play in Blue.

There was a Met Police Youth team. So a win there (with all credit to Graham Heath for this one) was one of those rare occasions when you don't mind taking 3 points from the police!

A win at Acton & Ealing Whistlers ushered in chants of "You're not whistling any more!" We whistled The Whistlers out of the Middlesex County Cup – which always had its fair share of interesting names. TFA (or Total Football Academy) came from Crouch End, Kodak Youth FC from Harrow, and Eagles United from Kosovo were, in fact, based in Golders Green.

Another we came across was St Gregory's, who described themselves as "a friendly football club run by parish parents." We hit 12 goals past them, one for each disciple, but sadly only one parish parent was there to witness it. And he'd driven his team bus to the wrong location. Talk about lost sheep.

⚽

Referencing the professional and Premier League game, and drawing parallels (however tenuous) was always a rich source of match reporting material. The parallel universe could provide some great analogies. Epsom Eagles were the Manchester United of the Epsom & Ewell league; Molesey Juniors the Real Madrid of U10 football; and playing away at Bedfont was like visiting the Britannia or the Reebok – it was all about grinding out a result.

The parallels between Newcastle United and NPL always intrigued me. There was a time when I concluded that both were directionless, and both were prone to losing. Newcastle went through an emotional roller coaster with Kevin Keegan, and NPL with Steven Bates. Newcastle had a Wise at the time (Dennis Wise, an ill-fated appointment as Executive Director of Football) and NPL a Wisdom (Stuart Wisdom, the NPL Chairman).

In the season that Newcastle had 4 managers (Keegan, Kinnear, Hughton and Shearer), so did NPL (Stuart, Paul, Martin and Steven). But while The Toon were relegated that season, the mighty NPL still managed a 4th place finish in the Premier League. It took several years longer on Tyneside.

At the beginning of one season, and after a poor start by Arsenal, Robin Brown decided that he would be focusing his emotional commitment on kids' football that year. As a Newcastle fan, enduring 14 years of Mike Ashley's club ownership, I had felt that way for many years. Sunday mornings were a welcome relief.

As an U17 team, we began competing in the same league as the NPL U18 team. So that gave us a great local derby. City v United, Celtic v Rangers, Everton v Liverpool, Tottenham v Arsenal, Newcastle v Sunderland, Fenerbahce v Galatasaray… or maybe this was more akin to AC Milan v Inter Milan, with Fortress NPL as our very own San Siro. There was no better place to play football on a Sunday morning. Sun shining, touchline banter, and a bowling green of a pitch for a tasty NPL v NPL local derby.

Goalkeeping feats could conjure up memoires of former greats. A Roundshaw keeper, making save after stunning save, was the equivalent of the Polish "Clown" Jan Tomaszewski, thwarting England's World Cup qualification hopes at Wembley in 1973. Meanwhile Max was able to pull off a Gordon Banks quality save, somehow touching a certain goal onto the crossbar – remember Pelé in Mexico, at the World Cup in 1970?

Sometimes, the parallels were more tenuous, such as when trying to justify a Cup defeat to a higher-ranking league team. One tie pitted Elm Grove Colts, the 3rd placed team in the top league (so at that time, the equivalent of Chelsea) against our

NPL boys, then the 3rd placed team in the third division (the equivalent of Hartlepool). So, although we lost the game, we were the "Pride of Hartlepool" – and we sure gave "Chelsea" a run for their money!

⚽

One vital role of the youth football match reporter is to find the positives – or even to make positives out of negatives. This was especially important when the boys were younger, and struggled to accept defeat, let alone criticism. I was the man with the rose-tinted glasses, tasked with finding reasons to be cheerful, wherever possible. I was the Peter Mandelson of the operation, finding the positive spin.

So, after a 10-1 defeat at South Park Juniors, as we long-suffering Toon fans tell one another on a regular basis, we have to "keep the faith!" Where were the positives? Look carefully, and you'll find them...

- The sun was shining.

- The Sergeant-Major cut a resplendent figure in his line-running lycra.

- Steven was very calm, and didn't attack any opposition players or officials.

- Alex Cozens, chasing a 40:60 through ball, made such an impact on their keeper that he got subbed off.

- Charlie played with the sort of heart and soul that Tim Blackman puts into haranguing referees.

- Max started using his mouth on the pitch – not just off it.

On another occasion, we lost 8-0, our worst defeat of the season. But there were still some strong positives to take from the game. Like our post-match penalties. Desperate to re-live his former glories, Kim "The Cat" Cheah went into an adult-sized goal, challenging the NPL players to beat him from the penalty spot. To the delight of the watching parents, Kim was unable to stop (or even get near) one single penalty…

The pint was always half full. In fact, after one defeat, we dropped to sixth place in the Premier League. But that meant we were still the sixth best team out of five Epsom & Ewell Under 11 divisions, or 52 different teams. By my mathematics, that meant we were in the top 12%. Maybe the pint wasn't half full after all… it was 88% full.

CHAPTER 13

BOYS ON TOUR

"You're never too old for a boys' trip."

There's something special about going away on tour, as a team. The adventure, the shared experience, and the heightened sense of belonging. It's like going away to watch England in a major tournament, with all your mates, or even Newcastle in Europe in the Champions League. Special and memorable moments.

Denis was the first to bravely take our (then still very young) Hampton Rangers boys on tour. Yorkshire was chosen as the venue, because new signing Ben King's father (the aforementioned Big Roger) had moved down from God's own country, so he had contacts up there, and could arrange a couple of fixtures. We dropped the boys off with Denis at the usual meeting place, the back streets of Oldfield Road in Hampton. Samuca, our star striker, had 3 holdalls full of deodorants, and nothing much else. And Denis, unused to taking 10- or 11-year-old boys away, had no Calpol; in fact, he had never even heard of Calpol, so we rushed back to equip him with a few bottles.

⚽

But they survived Yorkshire, so by the time Eduardo joined the set-up a few years later, we were going into Europe. Spain was chosen as the destination for our 2005 tour, and Edu's planning and execution was just magnificent. We took 17 boys (by then c15-year-olds) and 10 adults to Barcelona, Valencia and Lleida, to play in two tournaments against Spanish opposition, including the Valencia Under 15 Academy side. Edu arranged trips around both Barcelona's Nou Camp and Valencia's Mestalla Stadiums, and organised everything from travel, accommodation, leisure and sight-seeing activities, through to setting up a whole range of sponsorship deals. He even produced some English to Spanish key phrases for the boys, including chat-up lines such as, "Do you have a boyfriend?" and "You have beautiful eyes!"

The first minor hiccough was when we discovered that Samuca, who was still our star striker, had no documentation permitting him to travel – so tactical reorganisations were required, and the deodorants were left in Hampton. We arrived in Spain to be met by our own tour bus or coach, complete with Hampton Rangers Junior Football Club signage, and our very own coach driver. We doled out the room keys, at The Holiday Inn in Valencia, with the boys and parents sharing double rooms. There were only 3 rooms left, and 4 of us still to be allocated: Denis, Edu, me and the coach driver. Denis had by now been re-branded as El Presidente, so he had to have his own room. And none of us knew the coach driver, so he did too. That left me to share with the Spanish Maestro – and I have never known anyone with such an elaborate cosmetic and hair-styling routine. Every morning I learned new skills and tricks that I never knew I needed – and still don't.

Taking a large group of 15-year-old boys away to Spain for a week does raise one or two disciplinary conundrums – especially as 2 or 3 of our boys were renowned rule-breakers. That's when Big Roger came into his own. As someone who worked professionally with young offenders, he sat everyone down, and got out a flipchart. What standards and behaviours did everyone think should be allowed on tour, and what was not permissible and should not be tolerated? He then typed out the resultant tour charter, and got everyone to sign up to their own self-agreed rules. The theory was great, and most of it worked in practice too. But, after some anti-social behaviour by some of the boys in public, it didn't stop one of the traveling mums, Janet, to announce to the whole group that she was just "sooo embarrassed!"

Edu had encouraged the much-talking Henry Langford, our midfield general, to record a tour song, making him believe this was a Spanish tradition for touring teams. Henry was in a band, and a talented vocalist too, so he produced a version of Queen's *We Will Rock You*, set to new words:

Buddy, you're a boy, make a big noise:
You're going to take on the Spanish some day:
You got mud on your face, you big disgrace,
Kicking your ball all over the place...

Our tour anthem song was played in the coach, as we travelled around, taking in Las Ramblas, the Olympic Stadium at Montjuic, Valencia's Science & Art Museum and the Universal Port Aventura theme and leisure park. When we got to Lleida, we were hosted by Edu's parents, at their wonderful Meson Encantado restaurant. Edu's father served amazing local food, while Edu's mother washed the kits, and showed us photos of the young Master Rubio.

Edu was very close to playing professionally at Valencia, and indeed was Assistant Coach at their Academy before he came to England, and Hampton Rangers. So we trained at Cracks FC, a feeder and development centre for Valencia, and we then played a highly competitive match against the Valencia

U15 Academy side, for the Turia Cup. Edu clearly wanted to put down a marker, so he started William Hodgson, aka The Mighty Hodge, as our Enforcer or Destroyer in midfield – with instructions to kick, block and ruffle up a few Academy feathers. Will delivered, although we were still soundly beaten.

With Edu generating press reports and coverage from his local contacts, we travelled on to Lleida, where we competed against 2 other Spanish sides for the Terra Firma Cup. The games were tight and competitive – so much so that poor Nat, one of our squad players, had a minor panic attack when he was asked to warm-up and come on! He stayed on the bench, as we won the Cup, with an amazing Edu free-kick routine, straight off the training field. Our centre forward, Ed, peeled off the end of the opposition's wall, to receive the ball unmarked in space, and slot home to win the Cup.

There was a special announcement on the flight home, congratulating Hampton Rangers on winning the inaugural Terra Firma Cup, and some great video footage of El Presidente Denis, drinking champagne from the Cup. It was a first-class tour, and we even produced a DVD as a memento, "Viva El Rangers", heeding Denis's sage advice, "Just don't put too much of the football in there!"

I have very few regrets in life overall, but one of them is not going on our second Spanish Tour, which took the team to Galicia in northwest Spain 2 years later, in 2007. Running my own business, I felt I had to take a project from our major client, Bacardi – which meant running a workshop in Miami. But in retrospect, it was the wrong decision. How much more rewarding would it have been to be on tour with Hampton Rangers in Spain again?

⚽

We were less continental with NPL, so it was Butlins in Bognor in 2011. On the footballing side, there was a sense of déjà vu. With shades again of Italia 1990 (Torino) and Euro 1996 (Wembley), it was a semi-final defeat on penalties at Butlins 2011 (Bognor).

But there were plenty of off-pitch highlights, which there always are. Big Adam surprised us all with his Elvis karaoke number, "Hunka Hunka Burning Love." Kim Cheah provided a magnificent banquet of Chinese food for 20 people – and then promptly cleaned up on the poker table; (a big lesson learnt by "Page 19" Martin: never gamble with the Malaysian master). And Heurelho Gomes, then of Tottenham, was on prize-giving duty – causing much excitement for some of the boys, and grown adults too.

⚽

Next up it was Torquay in 2012 – the "Don't Mention the Score" Tour, which had even Basil Fawlty Bates smiling. It was caravans, which weren't exactly glamorous. In fact, it made us pine for Butlins. So we couldn't really blame Steven Holmes for sneaking off to Torquay's Grosvenor Hotel for dressed crab and lobster... or could we?

It was certainly a tour full of surprises – not least our crowning accolade, which saw our manager, The Bates-Meister General, and his captain, Kailan, picking up the Fair Play and Sportsmanship awards... Miracles clearly happen in Torquay!

Other tour highlights included the heavily bearded Hells Angels referees; Steven's motivational speech about what it means to wear the blue shirt of NPL ("this isn't playground football"); and Steven's subsequent post-match debrief: "If you snooze, you lose..."

Meanwhile, off the pitch, Kim was resplendent in a Chairman Mao hat – ordering £150 worth of Cantonese food, in his best and most fluent Cantonese; the sponsor funded garlic bread, chicken nuggets and chips for everyone during the Cup Final (dressed crab and lobster guilt-trip, maybe); and Big Adam arrived for Match of the Day with his Mighty Meaty pizza. The manager took his team on the scary Paignton seafront ride; Ella Heath (a long-suffering sister) survived watching 2 days of football, to get her trip to Paignton Zoo; and the NPL boys disrupted the awards ceremony with some Torquay Joke Shop stink bombs.

⚽

If good things come in threes, then after Bognor Regis and Torquay, it had to be The Isle of Wight in 2013. The "It'll Be Alright on The Wight" Tour.

By now, some familiar themes were taking hold. Big Adam's XL mixed grill heralded the start of the tour at the ferry port – before he showed the kids how to operate an amusement arcade. Keith's woolly mammoth hat wrested the headgear mantle from Chairman Mao – while his younger son Ted tried to keep warm on the touchline: it was freezing on The Isle of Wight. Tour Leader Lisa, one of the mums, forgot the NPL pennants, but was still happy to pose with the opposition's tassels. And Kim started the tenpin bowling with 2 'strikes', going on to register a top score of 153… who would bet against him?

Kailan won the Yorkshire pudding eating contest (with 5) at the all-you-can-eat Sunday lunch carvery – described as "the best £10 I've ever spent" by Bramhall Senior. And some unnamed NPL players put birdseed on the manager's caravan roof, to ensure he was up with the larks. Boys on tour, eh?

EPILOGUE

WHAT HAPPENED NEXT?

"They think it's all over! It is now!" – Kenneth Wolstenholme,
1966 World Cup Final commentary.

So, the boys all grew up, and it was the end of a wonderful era. 25 years on a touchline came to a close, at the final NPL Awards night. Everyone was out in force, and nobody wanted to go home. "Don't take me home," as the football chant goes.

When I look back now, it's incredible how much affection, emotion and loyalty was crammed into those 25 years. People joined our football clubs, and they tended to stay. Many people think the grass is always greener elsewhere, and I've always found it rather hypocritical when Premier League players look to move on, saying, for example, that they want to play Champions League football. If they're so talented, then why don't they help their current club qualify for Europe? We were lucky, and maybe skilled as well, in keeping so many players and parents together across so many years. This created a real team mentality, with shared values and many memorable experiences.

⚽

Jack and Will both kept playing football – and indeed they still do to this day. Team sports like football offer a ready-made social introduction in life, whether at university, work or in the community.

After university, Jack started playing for a Newcastle team called The Hustlers. To call them a pub football team may be a little harsh, though they were certainly sponsored by the local brewery. There were some talented players, like Chris Murphy, who had scored more goals at Wallsend Boys Club than Alan Shearer, and played for the Celtic Academy. And there were many more less talented players, but highly committed, nonetheless. Jimmy Beck, the right back from Northern Ireland, took his father's advice head-on. When Wesley told him to "hit the winger hard" early on, Jimmy did just that. It was a straight red card. Davey was the left back, ex-Army, having served on tours of duty in The Falklands and Afghanistan. Davey was short, stocky and 100% robust. When on a rare overlap, he went in to challenge his winger with a full-blooded shoulder barge, only for the quick-thinking winger to step out of the way. Davey just ended up hurling himself into touch.

Will started playing for Newcastle University's 1st XI, and a special moment for me was seeing my 2 boys (with an 8-year age gap between them) lining up together as centre backs, with Will putting in a guest appearance for The Hustlers. He was brought on at half-time, to partner his big brother, and Jack's team-mates had never seen him raise his performance so dramatically. He played like a man possessed – as Will pulled the strings and barked out instructions to everyone. Will now works at Sky in Sports, alongside one of his ex-NPL colleagues from years gone by, Alex Cozens. And Will shares a house in Clapham with 3 of his school footballing mates; after a teenage holiday there, they're still collectively known as The Malia 4.

It's incredible to see Eduardo, once of Hampton Rangers, now live on TV with West Ham United, as a first team coach in the Premier League. It's also great to see Steven Bates still plying his trade, and passing on his pearls of wisdom, as Academy Manager at Hampton & Richmond Borough FC.

As for me, I now get my footballing kicks at Newcastle United – with a season ticket meaning every home game at St James's Park is a 600-mile round trip from Hampton. But I now have 2 little grandchildren up in Whitley Bay to visit when I'm up there – and both Arabella and Alfie are already wearing the black and white stripes, and beginning to kick footballs and join clubs such as Little Kickers. Mia's boyfriend Conor is a PE teacher and football coach too. So who knows, could the cycle be starting all over again?!

THE CREDITS: MANAGERS & PLAYERS

**Hampton Rangers –
Managers & Coaches**
Denis Chaplin
Eduardo Rubio
Steven Higgins
Andy McLaren
Craig Wildy

Hampton Rangers – Players
Jack Christophers
Simon Veasey
Joe Patten
Jonny Williams
James Adams
Will Hodgson
Tom Jones
Oli Gibson
Stuart McLaren
Aaron Bryant
Calum Manson
Felix Chow
Henry Langford
Joe Snape
Ben Naughton-Rumbo
Alex Ramsay
Dan Hughes

Brook Driver
Vishal Makol
Ed Higgins
Samuca Coker
Ben King
Nat Jowitt
Will Kearney
Fred Parker
Max Ward
Matt Pursey
Caine Marshall
Tristan Loffler
Joe Barwick
Andrea Caio
Bobby Khangurra
Ash Amhama
Andrew Holder-Ross
Mark Goodman

**NPL Youth –
Managers & Coaches**
Steven Bates
Simon Worsfold-Gregg
Paul Brooker
Adrian Sandy
Barry Ruse

Stuart Ridgers
John Power
Martin Upson

NPL Youth - Players
Will Christophers
Joe Bates
Sam Cheah
Henry Newton-Savage
Theo Osborne
Owain Newman
Sam James
Jake Ruse
Tom Ridgers
Callum O'Reilly
William Westland
Mason Worsfold-Gregg
Luke Brooker
Alex Brown
Josh Blackman
Max Bramhall
James Meadows
Alex Cozens
Tom Tosetti
Alfie Ratchford
Luca Poulton
Ted Goodson

Kieran Power
Alex Sealy
William Hall
Mohammed Midiaf
Kailan North
Chris Wort
Charlie Holmes
Ellis Nicholls
Luca Tillot
Alex Green
Yousef Hedfi
Alfie Pope
Liam Heath
Alex Pearson
Ryan David
Dean Byne
Kai Hanley
Abs Rajab
Darcy Lewis
Josh Thompson
Will Davey
Callum Castling
Charlie Pike
Jack Smith
Ben Gallifent
Lewis Gallifent

WITH THANKS

With many thanks to those who have read and commented on early drafts, and for their encouragement and advice – Jack, Will, Rachel, Steven and Eduardo.

Also to Helen, for challenging me by asking who would ever want to read this book, and have I included too many rhetorical questions? I appreciated the irony of both comments.

Many thanks to Craig for legal advice, Jess for production, and Chloé for design.

And to all those players, parents and volunteers who contributed so much to those 25 years, making some very special memories together!